EXCHANGE OF HEARTS

N.R. WALKER

COPYRIGHT

Cover Artist: Sara York
Editor: Labyrinth Bound Edits
Exchange of Hearts © 2015 N.R. Walker
Publisher: BlueHeart Press

DEDICATION

For those who believe dreams aren't just for the dreamers.

EXCHANGE OF
Hearts

♫

N.R. WALKER

CHAPTER 1

SYDNEY

I WALKED side by side with the blonde, well-dressed woman and ignored the looks and laughter from the other guys.

Along with our student advisor, Miss Goff, I'd been relegated as the welcoming committee to the new kid. As part of a student exchange program, a kid from England was joining the ever-so-prestigious St Michael's Boarding School for three months.

So, why me? Why did I get picked to go?

Because he was going to be my roommate. That was why.

As we got to the car, Miss Goff stopped. "Oh, I just remembered I left the file in my office. I'll be right back, Harrison," she told me. "Wait here. I won't be a minute."

As she turned and walked briskly back toward the building, I leaned against the car, knowing the other kids would soon start with the slurs and teasing. I looked up, and of course it was *him* I saw.

"Have fun with Miss Goff," Carson taunted me suggestively. The other boys laughed. *His* personal entourage, of course they laughed. They were all rugby players, and I was the music nerd. Tall and thin, my dark hair made my skin look paler than it really was, with long piano-playing fingers, and I was usually alone—I was the opposite to their athletic builds and jock-pack mentality. Carson laughed the loudest. "No making out with the teacher at the airport, Haddon."

I didn't even bother with a comeback. I mean, why fucking bother?

He knew damn well she wasn't my type.

She. No, *shes* were not my type at all.

He knew this. He knew it damn fucking well. Because *he* and I had fooled around together. On the quiet, of course. In the darkened privacy of his room, only when *he* was certain there was no one else around, when it suited *him*.

Just kissing mostly, rubbing, dry humping—whatever the fuck you wanted to call it.

Making out. First base. Whatever.

It was after our last encounter that things changed.

It was about two in the morning and we'd been making out in his bed. We were both so hard, and he was whining and moaning as we writhed against one another. So I slipped my hand under the waistband of his boxers, and I gave him a hand job.

Skin on skin.

I wrapped my hand around his dick, pumped and squeezed him, and not a moment later he came.

It was the fucking hottest thing. Ever.

But afterwards, when his mind had cleared of his jizz-high, he was... different. He pulled away from me and suggested coldly I go back to my room.

It was too real for him.

I figured he just needed a day or two and then things would go back to normal.

But they didn't. They got worse.

The jokes, the taunting. It had been over three months now, and he still made fun of me. Although I could see it in his eyes, as he was saying hurtful things, his eyes were saying sorry.

And I couldn't bring myself to say anything back. I just... couldn't.

"You ready, Harrison?" Miss Goff's voice startled me. She had a manila folder in her hand. "We'd better go if we're going to be there when the plane arrives. We don't want to be late."

After we got into the car, she handed me the folder and then pulled out onto Ryde Road traffic, heading toward the city. I held the folder in my hands, not even bothering to open it. I couldn't care fucking less about some foreign exchange student. If I had to put up with a roommate, I didn't want to look at his face for any longer than necessary.

Miss Goff sensed my mood. "Don't worry about those boys," she told me. "People like Carson Sinclair aren't worth your time."

I snorted. If only she knew.

We drove for a few minutes in silence. Then she asked, "How's the music coming along?"

We discussed my music for the rest of the drive. It was an easy subject for me, my love of piano, even though she knew I couldn't make a career out of it. But thankfully before too much longer, we were walking into Sydney Airport's International terminal.

I figured this kid would take a while to get through customs and there'd be some kind of paperwork to fill out—I was also guessing you couldn't just walk into the airport and take some random kid. So presuming it was gonna take a while, I told Miss Goff, "I'm just going to grab a Coke. Can I get you anything?"

She was distracted enough, double-checking the board of flight numbers and arrival gates, and without looking at me, she shook her head. "No, thank you," she said, before reminding me, like I was five years old and not eighteen, not to wander off, not to go too far, and to come straight back.

I grabbed a drink, and keeping an eye on Miss Goff every now and then, I browsed through magazine racks. There was nothing really worth looking at—a nice one with Hugh Jackman on the cover, but I noticed two guys near the wall looking at a map. Obviously backpackers or hikers or something. They were dressed in cargos and T-shirts, hiking shoes; young, fit, healthy.

Hot.

I picked up a magazine and pretended to read it, but really I was just checking the two guys out. I didn't often get the opportunity to perv on guys, so I took my time.

Only they caught me staring, smiled politely and moved on. They walked past some other guy who seemed to have been watching me watching them, because he was trying not to laugh.

He was cute too; tall as me, blond-brown messy hair, blue eyes, pale skin, and his pink lips gave him a nice smile. He looked fit but not like the football meatheads back at school.

I wasn't embarrassed to have been caught looking—even in full school uniform, no one here knew me, and Miss Goff was nowhere in sight. So I decided to play it up. I looked him up and down, shrugged one shoulder, gave him one raised eyebrow and half a smirk.

He grinned, then turned his head quickly like someone called his name.

Exactly like someone called his name.

Like Miss Goff.

Fuck.

Oh, you have got to be fucking kidding me!

That was *him*?

My roommate for the next three months was the guy I just checked out?

I watched—like a slow motion car crash—as Miss Goff greeted him and offered to take his suitcase. She looked up, saw me, and called me over. His eyes followed hers, and when he saw it was me, his eyes widened, and he grinned like the Cheshire fucking cat.

I stuffed the magazine back in the rack and walked over, wishing the world would end in the next two seconds.

No such luck.

"Levi Aston?" Miss Goff said.

"Yes, Miss," he said with a posh British accent and a smile.

She grinned. "We'd like to welcome you to Sydney, Australia. St Michael's is proud to have you," she said. Then she looked at me, "This is Harrison Haddon. He's a boarder. He'll be your roommate and can show you around the school."

Levi extended his hand and looked at me with a knowing smirk. "Hello, Harrison."

Fuck. My. Life.

"Hello," I said, shaking his hand for as long as was considered polite, then let it drop.

I was in such deep shit.

CHAPTER 2

I'D ONLY HAD to take one look at this guy to know he'd be in with the cool kids: good looking and rich looking. Carson, he'll be in with Carson and his circle of friends. And I just fucking openly checked him out and checked out other guys in front of him.

These last few months of school, the most important, were going to be hell.

Miss Goff looked at me for a long second. "You okay there, Harrison? Look a little pale."

"I'm fine," I lied.

"Okay," she said, easily enough convinced. "I'll just go and finalize this paperwork." Then she left me alone with the exchange student. I looked anywhere but at him.

"You don't have to worry." His smooth English voice was soft. "I won't tell anyone, if that's what you're worried about."

I looked at him then. He looked sincere enough, but then he smiled and I didn't know if he was joking.

I decided to play dumb. "Won't tell anyone about what?"

He studied me, his eyes darted between mine, and after a while he said, "Nothing."

Considering he was my roommate for the foreseeable future, I figured I might as well try and be civil. I cleared my throat. "How was your flight?"

"Long," he answered with a smile. Then he looked me up and down. "Nice uniform," he said, still grinning.

I rolled my eyes. "Glad you like it," I said, smiling back at him. "Because you'll be wearing one just like it for the next three months."

He groaned, just as Miss Goff walked back. "Okay," she told us. "We're good to go."

Levi picked up his bags and we headed out into the cool July winter. Miss Goff made small talk about the weather; Levi left behind a warm summer, but London summers and Sydney winters weren't too different, apparently.

On the drive back to school, Miss Goff pointed out the Sydney Harbour Bridge and the Opera House, though I stared at the grey skies, wondering how these next three months would go. I only had four months to go of high school, and I had an awful sense of dread they were going to be miserable.

As we drove into the school grounds, Levi seemed pleasantly surprised. The old, prestigious buildings were steeped in history and the grounds were immaculate. I remembered my first impression of this place six years ago: I was intimidated by the sheer size of it, its age, and its beauty.

"So this is it," Miss Goff said. "St Michael's. Home sweet home, for the next three months anyway."

"It looks a bit like my old school," he said, staring up at the old stone church.

Miss Goff suggested I show Levi our room so he could

drop his bags off and get settled in. "Come back down to the main office in an hour," she said before leaving us alone.

I nodded toward the dorm, and I took his smaller carry-on bag, leaving him with the bigger suitcase as we walked up the two flights of stairs. "Thanks," he said. He seemed genuine, though my defences were up from what happened at the airport. I was waiting for the other shoe to drop, for the inevitable teasing to start. With a deep breath, I opened the door to my room, which was now *our* room. It was quite nice for a boarding school dorm. Seniors got bigger rooms—some shared, some didn't. I'd had the room to myself for the first five months of the year, and given the exchange program was only for three months, I should have the space back to myself with enough study time for my final exams.

There were two single beds, and I'd moved all my things on one side of the room. I put his carry-on on the other bed. "This is yours," I said. "I only ever used to put books on it."

Levi dropped his suitcase on the bed and looked around, seemingly pleased. It was easy to see he was excited —new country, new city, new school. He *should* be excited, and I tried not to let my sullen mood dampen his high. The sullen mood I'd been in for weeks....

I mean, it certainly wasn't Levi's fault I let Carson Sinclair break my heart.

So despite our less-than-stellar start, I decided I'd try and get along. And once he'd put his things away, I suggested I show him around the school. And as we walked and talked about his school in London, what music he liked, what he wanted to do and see while he was in Australia, I realised he was actually a really nice guy—he was smart and funny. I thought we could actually get along. I thought we could even be... well, friends.

"I have a sister Lila and a brother Jared. They're both

older than me and reckon I'm spoiled," he said with a laugh. "They're totally right, but I'm not complaining. Mum and Dad both work. Dad's an architect and works right in the city. He's pretty good at what he does apparently. Mum's a receptionist at a health clinic, but really she just loves looking after us."

"Did you board at your school?"

"Nah, not sure I could have handled living at school two four seven, three six five." He must have seen the confusion on my face because he added, "Twenty-four hours a day, seven days a week, three hundred and sixty-five days a year."

I snorted. "Right."

He smiled and I couldn't help but notice his alabaster skin and pink lips. "Anyway," he went on to add, "we didn't live too far away, and Mum couldn't stand the thought of us eating someone else's cooking everyday."

"How is she coping with you coming here?"

"Eh," he shrugged. "She cried. A lot."

"Your school was pretty posh, yeah?"

He nodded. "I suppose. It's not Eton or anything, but it's pretty good." We rounded the corner to the indoor pool, and I held the door open for him. He waited for me to join him before he asked, "So, what about your family?"

I repressed a sigh. "I have a younger sister, Holly. She goes to Riverdale Girls School, which isn't too far from here," I told him.

"Oh, your folks don't live close?"

I gave him a tight smile. "Actually they live about fifteen-minutes drive away, and I'd like to think we board so we can concentrate on our schoolwork, but really I think it's because having kids around the house is an inconvenience."

Levi stopped walking and stared at me. "Oh, man, that sucks."

I shrugged and laughed it off. "Don't stress. It's certainly nothing new to me."

"What do they do?" he asked, his eyebrow furrowed. "You know, for coin?"

"Dad's a doctor at St Alfred's Hospital," I said, carefully omitting the fact he was chief of staff and head cardiac surgeon. "And my mother just keeps herself busy on a dozen different committees, if only to keep her social calendar full."

"Oh."

"Do I sound bitter?" I asked with a laugh. "Anyway, this is the pool area, and there's a gym through there." I pointed to a door off the sidewall. "As a boarder you're allowed to use these facilities as you like."

"Okay, cool. Thanks."

I thought I might as well ask him the dreaded question —to determine which group of friends he'd fit in best with. "So, do you um, play any sport?"

He gave a shrug. "Nah. Played a bit of cricket, but just for fun. Not really my thing."

It was ridiculous how relieved I was. I was waiting for the word 'rugby' to come out of his mouth and for him to ask where the fields were and for him to be someone else I had to avoid, but it didn't happen. I bit my lip so I wouldn't smile and looked at my watch instead. "We better get back to the office."

As we headed back to the admin block, we were both more comfortable with each other. I pointed buildings out, told him what the food was like and which teachers to stay on the good side of, and we were both smiling as we walked into the administration office.

Father Collin met us at the door. He was an older priest, a big man who I'd always liked. After welcoming Levi to the school and country, he explained he'd organized uniforms, and when the older man handed the pile of grey and navy over, Levi looked at me and grimaced.

I laughed, and Father Collin asked, "Aren't you supposed to be in class, Mr Haddon?"

"I was given the day leave, Father," I explained. "As he'll be my roommate, I'm to show the new student around, get uniforms and timetables."

"Ah," he said, distracted. "Timetables." He picked up some papers and handed one to Levi. Then Father Collin said, "Mmm, looks like you two have some classes together." He looked at Levi. "Yes, Harrison will be more than helpful."

Levi smiled and glanced at me. "I'm sure he will."

Other students came into the office behind us, and Levi and I moved to one side to collect his things. He whispered, "Are all the teachers here priests?"

I laughed. "Most of them."

Levi groaned. "Oh, God."

"We only say that at mass on Sundays," I joked, and Levi laughed.

As we turned to walk out of the office, I almost, literally, ran into Carson.

Fuck.

He looked from me to Levi. "So, you're the new exchange student?" he asked with a fake smile.

Levi introduced himself and I stepped back as they made small talk. Levi glanced at me and I pretended to be listening to what Father Collin was saying to someone else, but I knew Levi saw how uncomfortable I was near Carson.

I wished I wasn't. I wished I could look him in the eye,

and I wished I could say hurtful things back to him. I wish I had the guts to hurt him like he hurt me.

"Can I help you, Mr Sinclair?" Father Collin called out. Carson told Levi he'd see him around school.

Levi smiled politely. "Sure."

I held the door for him again, and we walked back to our room in an uncomfortable silence. When we were inside, he put his pile of uniforms on his bed and turned to face me. "What's up with that Carson guy?"

I shrugged. "What do you mean?"

He smiled but asked me quietly, "Does he pick on you?"

I shrugged again. "A little."

"I saw how you shrunk back from him. Wanna tell me why?"

"It's a long story."

"I've got three months," he said, not taking his eyes from mine. Then he tilted his head a little. "Does it have anything to do with you checking guys out at the airport?"

I was taken aback by his question, obviously unable to hide the vulnerability and truth flashing in my eyes.

He nodded. "So he's a homophobe, then? Gutless twat."

The words were out before I could stop them. "He's my ex."

Levi's eyes popped wide and his mouth literally fell open. "Really?"

I nodded and felt my cheeks flush. I'd never admitted this stuff to anyone. "Kind of." I sat on my bed and sighed. "We used to... do stuff... in his room. We were never boyfriends. We just... um...."

"Experimented?" he finished for me.

I nodded. "I've never told anyone. Not a soul. So please, please promise me—"

"I won't tell anyone," he said solemnly, and for whatever reason, I believed him.

He was quiet for a while, then he asked, "How did you get together? I mean, no offence, but he's a jock. And you're...."

"A geek?" I filled in the blanks.

He sat on his bed across from me. He chuckled and put his hand against his chest. "Yeah, from one geek to another, tell me how you bagged the jock?"

I snorted out a laugh and felt relieved in actually being able to tell someone what I'd kept secret for so long. "He and I were paired as chemistry lab partners. We had study sessions in his room...." I trailed off. I didn't need to explain, so I asked him something else instead. "Does it not bother you... that I like guys?"

He laughed. "Um, no. I like guys too. I mean, I lost my virginity with a girl," he said without shame. "But I've done stuff with guys too, and I've gotta say, I prefer the boy side of the fence."

I couldn't help but smile. "What was it like? Having sex with a girl?" Then I realised I'd just asked him something incredibly personal. My whole face burned. "Oh, um. You don't have to answer that."

He laughed. "Soft." Then his eyes widened. "No, not me," he barked out a laugh. "I was just fine and hard. I meant she was soft."

I laughed at that. "I knew what you meant."

"Oh," he said, grinning. "Have you been with a girl?"

"I've made out with a few girls, but not... sex," I admitted quietly.

"Have you had sex with a guy?" he asked, bright eyed. "You and Carson, did you...?"

I shook my head, silently admitting I was still a virgin. "We never got that far."

"Yeah, it's a pretty big step," he conceded. "What happened? Why'd you break up?"

So I told him. I told him how we'd been secretly seeing each other, making out, getting a little further each time. We'd made each other come before, but never skin on skin. I told him how he freaked out after I gave him a hand job and how he'd been cold and cruel toward me since.

"What a twat," Levi said.

"Yeah." I nodded. "It's kinda sucked."

"You liked him, didn't you?"

I nodded again. "I mean, I thought I did. But I've seen a side to him I don't like at all."

He settled down on his bed. "Do your parents know?"

My eyes bulged. "No. God, no." He nodded, in understanding, I thought. So I asked him, "Do yours?"

He made a face. "Yeah. But I lived at home with my folks. It's a bit different from being at boarding school."

I sighed. "Yeah, an old *Catholic* boarding school; old money, old traditions, old religion."

"Old priests," Levi added with a smile.

"Yeah, I somehow don't think they'd appreciate two of their students at an all-boys school hooking up."

He snorted. "Yeah, I don't think confession at mass would ever be the same."

I laughed, and talk turned to school subjects, and what we wanted to do when we graduated. I told him about my dad's expectations of me becoming a doctor. "Dad's a doctor, Grandad was a doctor," I said. "They both went to this school, too."

"Is that what you want to do?" he asked.

I sighed. "I could think of worse professions."

His lips twisted and I could tell he was deliberately choosing to not say something.

"What?" I prompted.

"Nothing, really," he said with a shrug. "I'm just a believer in doing what makes you happy, not what makes someone else happy."

"Yeah well," I replied, "you haven't met my dad. To him, my music is just a hobby."

"Music?"

I nodded. "Piano. Not a huge demand for classical pianists out there."

"You play classical?" He couldn't hide his surprise.

"Yeah, but only two units toward my HSC. Dad wouldn't let me take it as a three-unit elective. He said I had to concentrate on maths, physics, and chemistry to get me into med school." Levi frowned but said nothing. So I asked him, "What are you gonna do after school?"

"Architecture. I suppose I'm a bit like you in that it's what my dad does, but in my case, it's what I really want to do too. But I've actually already finished sixth form."

"You what?"

He grinned at my expression. "Two weeks ago. Our school years are different. I'm here to do my autumn term, but I've really finished already. My exams are done."

"If you're finished, then what the hell are you doing back at high school?"

He laughed. "My school offered a Study Abroad program, this was when I could fit it in around my A Levels," he said. "It's kinda like a holiday before starting uni."

"A holiday? You call coming back to high school a holiday?"

He laughed. "It is when you don't have to worry about grades."

I fell back onto my bed, but my feet were still on the floor. "Ugh. I wish I didn't have to worry about maths."

He laughed. "Maths was my favourite subject." I lifted my head and looked at him like he was crazy. He laughed at me and said, "I could help you, if you like. Like a tutor."

"You don't have to do that," I mumbled, letting my head fall back onto the bed.

"Think of it as payment for giving up your room. Because that must have sucked."

I laughed, relieved. I couldn't explain the relief. He was like me. In more ways than one. And I decided if he helped me with maths, then I got to hear his accent more often. "Deal."

CHAPTER 3

OVER THE NEXT FEW DAYS, Levi settled in okay. He slept a bit, but adjusted to the time zones okay, and didn't seem to mind the winter. He didn't even get lost once, and he found his way around on his own in no time. He even tried Vegemite on toast, but declared afterwards, adamantly, that there should be an international inquiry into how Australians could get Marmite so very, very wrong.

He had most of his classes with me, and he seemed to enjoy doing the work even though it had no bearing on his grades. And even the novelty of his accent had died off with the other students. Above all that, he seemed content to hang out with me.

I didn't mind. I didn't mind at all.

On the Friday after he arrived, Levi and I were leaving our last class of the day when half the rugby team ran past us, carrying school bags, obviously in a hurry.

"Where are they off to?" he wondered.

"The rugby league team has practice this afternoon," I told him.

He looked at me, with one eyebrow raised. "And you know this, how?"

"Carson plays. I used to watch him sometimes," I admitted. "I actually used to play, as a junior. St Michael's is big on football—it's like a nursery for scouting agents."

He blinked. "You played?"

I snorted. "I know, I'm not really built for it. But yes. More to fit in than anything else, but it really wasn't my thing."

"Shall we go watch them?" he asked, his eyes lighting up.

"You really want to?" God, I couldn't think of anything worse.

"Yep. I want to show you something."

Curious as to what he meant, I agreed. We dumped our bags and sat at the oval, with our jackets and scarves pulled high around our necks, and watched the two teams practise. Their faces were flush with cold, their breaths were puffs of steam, and they jumped and moved just to keep warm. Soon enough they were running, passing the ball, and practicing hit-ups. All the while Levi watched on. "God, this game makes absolutely no sense," he said. But then the team started stretching and bending over. Levi nudged me with his elbow and said, "But God, they're fun to watch."

I laughed at him. "What did you want to show me?"

"Carson," he replied.

"What?"

"He looks at you."

What? "No, he doesn't."

"Didn't you see him just now?" Levi asked. "When you laughed, he looked over at you. But not just now either. I mean, in class as well."

"That's bullshit."

Levi shook his head and watched as some of the younger players wrapped up their training session. The younger guys had to walk past us to get to the dressing rooms, and Levi talked into his scarf so only I could hear. He looked at me when he said, "I think someone might be a little jealous."

I looked from Levi to Carson and shook my head. It wasn't possible. But Levi nudged me again, and I couldn't help but smile. When I looked over at Carson, he was looking at us, trying not to look like he cared, but there was an edge to his eyes. *My God, I think Levi could be right.*

I glanced at Levi. "Do you think so?"

He nodded. "I know so." He went back to watching the guys still out on the field. After a while he asked, "Do you want him back? As your not-boyfriend?"

I followed his gaze to look at Carson, where he was still doing training. He was tall, good looking, with a thickset build and dark brown hair—there was no doubt the guy was hot. Even more so with his flushed cheeks and hard, short breaths. And I knew how hot he was underneath those clothes, and what he felt like in my hands. What he looked like when he came.

But I also knew how much he'd hurt me and just how cruel he could be.

"No," I answered honestly, quietly. "I don't want him back."

"Took a while to answer," Levi said with smiling eyes. "Are you sure?"

Just then the team finished training and started walking toward the dressing room and Levi did the unthinkable. "Hey Carson!"

"What the hell are you doing?" I hissed at him.

Levi just grinned underneath his scarf and when

Carson stopped in front of us, he said, "Looking good out there."

His compliment took Carson by surprise. "Uh, thanks."

Levi smiled. "So when's the game?"

"Two o'clock tomorrow," Carson answered.

"Oh, that's a shame," Levi replied. He looked at me, "We've already got plans."

No we didn't. Not that I recalled, anyway.

Levi looked up at Carson and smiled at him. "Maybe next time."

Carson eyed Levi cautiously, and I think he was trying to decipher Levi's sincerity. Then he looked at me for a long moment. He nodded, "Haddon."

He never used to address me by my surname. I returned the favour. "Sinclair."

His eyes tightened before he looked back at Levi. "Levi, you should hang out with us." He gave a nod to his entourage walking back to the dressing room. "Instead of wasting your time with... less important people."

Fuck. *Less important people.* Fuck, fuck.

Levi laughed and leaned back so his shoulder was closer to mine. "Thanks for the offer," he told him, still grinning. "But *Haddon* here," he nudged my shoulder with his, "well, he's got me covered," he said almost suggestively.

Carson's jaw clenched, and without a word, he turned and headed for the dressing rooms.

Before I could ask Levi what the fuck he thought he was doing, he laughed to himself. "What a wanker."

"Mmm," I agreed. "That's why I don't want him back."

Levi looked at me. "He's an arsehole to you. We should totally have some fun with him."

"What do you mean?"

"By making him jealous," he said with a grin. "Because

you have the upper hand." I looked at him like he'd lost his mind, and Levi shook his head. "Harrison, he wants you. Can't you see that?"

I remembered how he'd looked over at us. He had looked a little curious.

Levi just smiled and nudged me. "See?"

I chuckled, feeling a little embarrassed. "How do you go about making Carson Sinclair jealous?"

"*You* don't," he answered with a grin. "*We* do."

"What?"

"You saw how he reacted to seeing us together," he answered with a smirk.

"Oh no," I shook my head. "Levi, I can't come out just to get back at him."

He surprised me by laughing. "No, no. When no one else is around—just him—we play it up. Like we did just now; no one else heard anything. We won't have to even say anything outright, just hints."

He could see I was intrigued with the idea and he added, "No one else will know. I promise. It'll just fuck with his head."

Without giving him a direct answer, yes or no, I tightened my scarf and got to my feet. "Come on. I'm going to do laps."

"You swim?"

I nodded. "It clears my head." I very deliberately didn't tell him I also swam lap after lap to clear my head of the sex-filled thoughts that lived in my brain.

"It's freezing fucking cold," he cried.

I laughed. "The pool's inside, remember? And it's heated."

"Oh, well in that case, can I come?" he asked brightly. "I could do with a workout."

I TOLD him to pack some clothes for afterwards, his shower gear and towel. There was no point in getting changed twice, and we may as well have showers down there. We got down to E block and found the pool relatively empty. I tried not to watch him get undressed, very deliberately not looking at him as I changed.

"You swim often?" he asked.

I looked up at him then; he was wearing only swimming shorts. His long, lean body was so pale he was almost white, but he was toned. I made myself look at his face and he grinned.

I could feel my face heat with embarrassment, then remembered he asked a question. "Uh, yeah. I try to swim a couple of k a week."

His eyes raked down my body, and as he walked past me, he whispered, "I think I can tell."

By the time I'd composed myself enough to turn around, he was on the starting block, adjusting his goggles, but still grinning. He dived cleanly into the water and started swimming freestyle down the pool.

I took the lane next to his and dived in. As my body moved through the water, I found the concentration on my breathing relaxing, and all the clutter from my mind disappeared—school, exams, Carson, and now Levi. And by the time I felt the burn in my limbs and lungs, I must have done a dozen laps.

I pulled myself out of the pool to find Levi already towelling off. He was still wet, so he'd not been out long. He rubbed the towel over his hair, leaving it spiking up in all different directions. It made me want to touch it. "Feel better?"

"Yeah," I puffed. "You?"

He nodded, and before he could say anything else—or before I could lose my resolve, with Carson's words of *someone more important* still playing in my mind, I told him, "I want to do it. I want to get back at Carson."

He grinned, all wet blond hair and blue eyes.

"But," I stated my conditions, "it can't interfere with my studies, it won't get us into trouble, and no one else will know."

He laughed. "Deal."

CHAPTER 4

GIVEN it was a Saturday and we had the day to ourselves and didn't want to watch rugby, I took Levi into the city. We checked out Darling Harbour, the Harbour Bridge, and the Opera House. He did the tourist thing, taking photos and having me take photos of him.

We had a great time despite the cold weather, and the more we talked, the more we got along. We were just two guys, hanging out, having a laugh, but it wasn't lost on me how easy it was.

How easy it could be, to be hanging out with a boyfriend... if coming out wasn't so damn hard.

We stuck to ourselves over the weekend. Neither one of us mentioned Carson or the half-botched scheme to make him jealous, however preposterous it seemed.

But two days later, on Tuesday, it happened.

We walked into the library, to where the seniors have sectioned off areas for privacy. And Carson was there.

All by himself.

Levi led the way to a table, diagonally in front of Carson, so he *had* to see us. He pulled out two chairs, nodding to one, silently telling me to sit beside him. And once we'd got our books out in front of us, Levi put his hand on the back of my chair and leant right over to me.

I could feel the heat of his body, his breath on my neck. God, he was so close it made my chest tighten. Then he whispered, "See how easy it is? He's watching us right now." He smiled. "He can't take his eyes off you."

I could feel the heat of blush creep along my cheeks, and I let out a nervous laugh. When I snuck a glance over my shoulder, I could see Levi was right.

Carson was staring. More like glaring. I turned back around, fighting a smile. Levi sat back in his chair, and not a second later, Carson packed up his things and left.

As he disappeared through the door, I laughed.

"See? I told you," Levi said smugly.

"Maybe we shouldn't antagonize him," I said, though I couldn't stop grinning.

"What can he say? It's exactly like you said. You can't say anything without outing you both, and neither can he."

I nodded. "True."

Levi looked straight at me. "So, how'd it feel?"

I smiled at him. "It felt good."

Then slowly, he lifted his hand and touched my cheek. "And this blush... God, right on cue."

"I, uh...," I stammered and of course, blushed again. "I um, can't help that."

"It's beautiful," he said softly.

Fuck. My heart was pounding. "Um, trigonometry...?" I asked, though it was more of a squeak. I pushed the book on the table in front of us.

Levi smiled, turned in his seat, and we started going through our work, though I glanced at him every so often. I could feel my dick getting hard as my body reacted to him. I mean, fuck. I was eighteen years old. I had perma-wood on any given day.

At this rate, I was going to be doing a *lot* of laps.

OVER THE NEXT WEEK, Levi and I had classes together, we hung out together, and studied in our room together. He Skyped with his family some nights, and once he even dragged me over to say hello to his brother.

I found myself having to hide my ever-present erection from him—with my bag, my towel, the way I sat with my knees up. And when I wanked in the shower, the faceless guy who I used to imagine was doing it for me, now had a face. He also had blond-brown hair, blue eyes, and a British accent.

"Harrison?"

The way he said my name me shiver. "Yeah?"

"Did you zone out on me?" he asked with a laugh. "I've been explaining this math equation, and you're staring off in space."

"Sorry. I was a million miles away."

We were in our room, on our own beds, supposedly studying. Well, he was studying. I was fantasising about him whispering in my ear with that sexy accent of his. He sighed and, getting up off his bed, he crawled onto mine. He sat on the end with his back leaning against the wall, his book open in his lap. "Okay, so question fourteen..."

He was so close, almost touching me. I could smell his deodorant. I could feel the warmth of his skin. Somehow *almost touching* me was worse. It was static and dizzying. My heart rate hammered and my dick responded.

I sat up quickly, and like him, leaned against the wall.

But I grabbed my pillow and put it over my lap and opened my textbook on top of it, acting like it was just a more comfortable way to read, but really trying to hide my erection.

Fucking hell.

When I'd imagined the next three months would be torture, this was not exactly the punishment I had in mind.

"Comfy now?" he asked, a smirk pulled at his lips.

His soft-looking, plump pink lips.... My mind went straight to the gutter, and I imagined what they'd feel like, what they'd taste like, what they'd look like around my dick... *Oh fuck.*

"Um, yeah. I just need to take a bathroom break," I lied, scampering off my bed and rushing to the door. "Be right back."

I did actually go to the bathroom, but not to pee. I stood in the cubicle and tried to catch my breath. I had to find a way to stop this, because it was getting ridiculous. And embarrassing.

But it only got worse. Because that week, every opportunity where Carson was near us, Levi played him. He'd lean in close to me, whisper something in my ear, touch my arm, or even just look at me like he wanted to have me. He played his part perfectly. No one else noticed. But Carson did, and it was silently getting under his skin.

And as gratifying as that was, it was starting to mess with my head. And when I say mess with my head, I mean turn me on.

One afternoon after school, we walked down to the little supermarket not far from campus. It was the usual place boarders went to pick up snacks, drinks, and magazines. When we walked in, we found a few other guys there, Carson being one of them.

"Not here," I told Levi.

He nodded in understanding but seemed a little disappointed. And as we scouted through the aisles, it just so happened that Carson was there by himself.

Levi looked at me, but I shook my head no.

To his credit and my relief, he didn't say anything, or do anything, and we bought our stuff and went back to our room.

"That was the perfect opportunity!" he told me, dumping his things on his bed. "God, I could have had some fun with the cucumbers."

When I didn't laugh at his joke, he looked at me. "Harrison, what's up? Are you starting to have second thoughts?"

"It's not that," I said.

"Then what is it?" he questioned.

"Nothing," I lied. "It's just...." I didn't finish. I couldn't finish.

Levi walked over to stand right in front of me. "It's just what?"

I shook my head and took a step back from him, trying to put some distance between us.

"It's just what?" he said again, taking another step toward me.

"Um," I swallowed thickly, taking another step back. "Every time you... do something to piss Carson off... you...." God, I couldn't say this.

"I what, Harrison? Just tell me and I'll stop it."

"No," I blurted out. "I uh, I don't want you to stop it."

His eyes widened. He was confused, curious.

Oh, God. Oh, fuck. I could feel myself blush right down my neck. Considering what I'd said already, I may as well just finish and completely die of embarrassment. "Every time you do something to make Carson jealous... you... youmakemehard."

He blinked.

And I wanted to die.

He blinked again. Then a slow spreading smile took over his face. "I make you hard, huh?"

I breathed out shakily and nodded. "When you lean in and whisper... when you touch me...."

He was grinning now, right in front of me. I couldn't move; even if I could have made my legs work, I was backed in against my bed.

"Harrison," he said softly. He lifted his hand toward my face. "Can I touch you?"

I couldn't speak, so I swallowed and nodded. Then ever so softly, he touched his fingers to my cheek. He mumbled, and I could barely hear him over my pounding heart. "So beautiful."

I found myself smiling shyly at his words. God, I was never embarrassed like this with Carson, but something about Levi made me nervous. He was so close to me. His body, his face, his eyes, his mouth.

"I want to kiss you," he whispered.

I wanted to tell him yes, please, hurry-the-fuck-now, but I still couldn't speak. Instead my body moved of its own accord and I pressed my lips to his, taking him by surprise. I held his face in my hands, and I was urgent, trying to deepen the kiss.

He responded to me. His mouth opened and our tongues met, making us both groan.

And it was want and need, tongues and lips, pushing and pulling. His mouth was hot and sweet, and when he slid his arms around me and pulled us together, I almost buckled.

We fell onto the bed—I don't recall who led who—and he stopped kissing me and stared at me. We were both breathing hard, but his eyes were filled with questions. I nodded, so he knew I wanted this. Like it was all the answer he needed, he manoeuvred us so both of us were in better positions on our sides, and our heads were on my pillow.

Then he looked into my eyes and kissed me softly. It was slower now but deeper, more serious, and with a surety I didn't possess. Without breaking the kiss, he rolled us over and settled his weight on me.

It was divine.

He was in between my legs, his heavy weight, his hips, his hard-on.

I was moaning as we kissed; I knew it, but I couldn't seem to stop. And he seemed to like it, because he started to grind into me.

And I could feel his cock.

He was hard. *So* hard.

As was I. Achingly so.

He slid his tongue along mine as he ran one hand under my arse, pulling me up to him as he pushed his hips into me. And it was too much, yet still not enough. So I ran my hands down his back and squeezed his arse, and rubbed my erection against his.

And he moaned.

And it did me in.

Unable to hold back my orgasm, I bucked against him while holding him tight. The pressure against my cock sparked the pressure in my belly, in my balls, and I came so fucking hard.

He groaned at my release and kissed me, tonguing me thoroughly as my body shook underneath him. And then he reared up on his hands, pinning his hips into mine, grinding his cock against me so hard, and through his trousers I could feel his cock pulse and spill.

"Oh my God," I whimpered. I'd never felt anything like it. I'd never seen anything like it.

His face, as he came, was so tormented, yet so serene at the same time. And he thrust and trembled before collapsing on me. His face was buried in my neck. "Oh, Harrison, Harrison, Harrison." He murmured my name over and over.

And I started to laugh. I tried to hold it in, but he could feel my chest vibrate. He pulled his head back, still starry-eyed, and he looked at me. His out-of-focus eyes made me laugh some more.

And then he smiled and started to laugh too.

I lifted my head off the bed and pecked his swollen lips. "That was so fucking hot."

He barked out a laugh, then kissed me, open mouthed but soft enough to make me hum. I pulled my mouth from his and told him, "If you keep kissing me like that, I'll be ready to go again."

He groaned. "That's not a bad thing, believe me."

I laughed. "It is if I have to sit through dinner with a hard-on."

He bit his bottom lip. "I have, every fucking night, since I got here. And breakfast and morning classes and lunch and afternoon—"

I got the point, so with smiling lips I kissed him to shut him up. He laughed into my mouth. "It's true," he said, pulling away. "Since I first saw you at the airport."

I was smiling like a loon. "So the whole ploy with Carson wasn't really to make him jealous at all?"

He gasped, like he was offended, but his smile gave him away. "No, he's an arsehole, and he deserves to be shown what he's missing out on." He pecked my lips. Then he said quickly, "But it was a good plan, and I didn't mind acting like we were together."

I laughed some more, and shifted underneath him, becoming very aware that I was a sticky mess. That we both were.

"We should get cleaned up," I suggested.

He nodded and rolled off me, and after we'd cleaned up and redressed, we headed downstairs for dinner. It wasn't awkward between us like I thought it might be. In fact it was better. We still talked and laughed like we'd always done, but his eyes shone when he looked at me.

After dinner we hit the books, Levi on his bed, me on mine, until we kept looking over at each other getting no studying done. Levi threw his book on the floor and mumbled, "Fuck physics," then crawled up my body.

I laughed, threw my book so it landed somewhere near his, and slid my hands up his chest. We made out, kissing, nibbling ears, licking necks, and feeling every inch of clothed bodies our hands could reach.

He squirmed when I skimmed my hands along his ribs, he groaned when I palmed his arse, he grunted when I dug my fingers into the back of his denim clad thighs, and he gasped when I gently pulled my hands through his hair.

"Fuck," he mumbled. "You know what you're doing to me?"

I nodded. "I can feel it," I told him, lifting my hips to prove my point.

He kissed me deeply, fiercely, then pulled my bottom lip between his. "Can't get enough."

"Mmmm," I moaned. My whole body was warmed all over.

He shuddered and I palmed his dick through his jeans.

He quickly did the same to me, kissing, rubbing, moaning. Coming.

Needless to say, we didn't get a great deal of studying done. And we needed to do an awful lot of laundry.

THE NEXT FEW days were glorious. We went to class, we hung out, we studied, and at night, we made out.

"Ugh, so much laundry," he grumbled, looking at his pile of clothes.

"I think the laundry staff are wondering what we're doing," I agreed with a laugh.

"You know," he hedged, "we wouldn't have to do so much if we weren't wearing clothes."

I stared at him, and he bit his bottom lip. "And think of the water we'd save. It really is an environmentally sound thing to do."

He pulled my shirt over my head and skimmed his hand over my chest. With warm hands and confident fingers he explored my skin, and I was never going to say no. But then he undid my fly and slid his hand beneath my briefs. He was so sure, so assertive with what he wanted. When I was naked in front of him, he never took his eyes from mine. He never looked me over. He never broke eye contact. He was showing me he respected me, that I could trust him. And I did.

It was a little weird at first, both being naked on our knees, facing each other on his bed. His cock was uncut— different from mine—and I stared at it, at him. I wanted to do so much to him; I wanted to touch him, taste him, but I seemed to be frozen.

Then he started to stroke himself, sliding his hand down

his shaft, squeezing and twisting the head. And I moaned. I started to work my own cock, and he groaned, "Oh, is that how you like it?"

I tried to keep looking into his eyes, but couldn't take my eyes off his dick—how his hand moved, how his hips flexed, how the muscles slid under his skin.

When he used his other hand to grab my face and pull my mouth to his, it took me by surprise. He was kissing me so hard, so demanding—his tongue, his teeth. He gripped my face, around my jaw and my neck, and he moaned as he pumped himself harder, and then he came.

On me.

Hot, thick, and wet come splashed against my chest and stomach as he bucked and groaned. His kiss seemingly forgotten, I watched his eyes roll, and he moaned my name.

And my cock spilled, painting lines of come on his skin. Then he was kissing me again, plunging his tongue into my mouth and making my orgasm surge harder, longer.

We collapsed on each other, our bodies boneless and spent, skin sticky between us. He grinned as he wiped me clean with tissues and laughed as I overbalanced and almost fell off the bed.

And that week, while we didn't have an opportunity to be alone with Carson, there was the time in the lunch line where Levi did the eye thing. He just smiled, looked from me to Carson and back again. No one else noticed but me and Carson. Carson's jaw bulged a bit and he was quick to look away.

It was the week after that that we noticed Carson was avoiding us. Even when he walked past me in the hall with his friends, he didn't say a word to me. He didn't even look at me.

All the while, every night in our room, Levi and I made out, usually ending in us giving each other hand jobs.

It got to the point where my books were being forgotten, and Levi set a new rule: homework and study first, and if I spent any less than an hour every night doing homework, he wouldn't make me come.

I gave him a mock salute and rolled my eyes, but after an hour every night, when my time was up, I claimed my reward.

———

WHEN LEVI HAD BEEN HERE for four weeks, I took him to Taronga Zoo. "You can't come to Australia and not see kangaroos and koalas," I told him. So we started with the Australian animals, making our way around the Sydney landmark.

At one point he grabbed my hand to drag me toward the baby elephant enclosure, and he didn't let it go. We stood against the railing, our fingers entwined between us.

It was crowded. Most people were shoulder to shoulder, so we didn't look out of place. But I was holding hands with a guy in public.

My heart was pounding and I was smiling, but not at the cute baby elephant. Levi leaned against me. He squeezed my fingers and sighed.

And then he let go of my hand.

"Come on," he said with a smile, pointing to the sign. "Tigers are this way."

We spent the entire Saturday walking around the park, laughing and talking, and soon enough it was time to head back to school. We took the ferry back to the city, and as Levi fell into the seat next to me, he picked up my hand and dropped his head on my shoulder. "We must have walked miles," he said.

It was private in our seats, so I wasn't worried about being spotted. I squeezed his hand in mine, its warmth sent tingles through me, and I hummed. "Mmm, we did walk miles."

"Such a shame," he mumbled.

"Why?" I asked with a laugh.

"Because you'll be too tired to study for more than an hour."

The thought of what he was implying made me hum. "Never too tired for that."

He held my hand again on the bus from the city back to school. No one looked at us. No one cared. And I liked it. I wanted it to be a permanent thing. I wanted to be able to be myself. More than anything in the world, I wanted to be me, without fear of retaliation.

He rubbed his thumb over the back of my hand, and when I looked at him, he smiled. I grinned at him and I thought for a moment he was about to kiss me. On the bus. In front of everyone.

But he didn't.

And I didn't know if I was relieved or disappointed.

That night after dinner and showers, I did manage to study for an hour. And when I closed the book, he was watching me, waiting. I smiled at him. "You *that* keen to give me a reward for being a good boy?"

He bit his bottom lip, and he looked different. His eyes were darker, deeper, and it did something to my belly. He nodded and walked slowly over to me, put his knee on the bed and swung the other leg over me. It was heady enough that he was straddling me, but then he undid my jeans.

He didn't say a word. He just slipped his hand underneath my briefs and pulled me out. I was already half hard; it didn't take much—just a fucking look and he turned me on.

We shuffled back on the bed then, really slowly, he leaned down and licked me. Right there. At the tip. His tongue darted out and he tasted me.

"Sh—sh—sh—shit!" I whispered, jerking in his hand. "Levi, what are you doing?"

He smirked and did it again. With his tongue—*Ohmyfuckinggod. Oh, yesssssss.*—he licked me. The entire length of me.

And when I thought it couldn't possibly get any better, he opened his mouth and took me inside.

Warm.

Wet.

Hot.

Wet.

Sucking.

Ohmyfuckinggod, the sucking....

Somewhere in my brain screamed *open your fucking eyes and watch!*

So I did. *Oh, fuck, fuck, fuck.*

His lips were around my dick, his hand at the base, and then he looked up at me.

And I was done.

I couldn't hold back my release if I wanted to. I tried to warn him, "Le—Le,—Levi, come, come, coming...."

He pulled his mouth from me, my back arched off the bed as blissful heat ripped through my body, and come shot across my stomach.

I had no sight, no sound, no anything.

Just the feel of Levi's hand on my face as he gripped me,

pulling my mouth to his. And he kissed me, deeply, thoroughly, differently.

There was no chuckling, no laughing at ourselves. Just his body on top of mine, the taste of me on his tongue and my bones were warm jelly.

When I opened my eyes, I found his were still closed. He tilted his face to kiss me deeper. His invading tongue made my eyes roll.

He groaned into my mouth, pushing his hips into mine. I could feel how turned on he was, so with both hands, I pulled his face away. "Your turn."

"You don't have to," he said with swollen lips.

"I want to," I told him honestly. "I want to taste you."

He shuddered and I flipped him over, and once I was kneeling between his legs, I undid his jeans.

I took his hard cock out of his briefs and pumped him a few times. "I've never done this before," I told him, but I leaned down and swiped my tongue across his head.

He flinched and hissed.

So I did it again. And again and again. I liked the taste of it, the musky, salty taste of him. So I licked his shaft and he groaned as his fingers slid into my hair.

This time I took him between my lips, and sucked on the head, like he just did to me. I flicked my tongue across him while I sucked, and his back arched and his hips flexed. "Fuck, Harrison," he groaned and fisted the blankets at his sides.

I took him a little deeper, sucked a little harder, and when I cupped his balls with my hand, he bucked again, trying to thrust into my mouth. "Fuck, coming," he cried.

I took my mouth off him—I wasn't ready for that—and I pumped him harder until he was shooting come all over his shirt.

He moaned as his entire body trembled—his thighs, his hands. It was beautiful to watch.

With a shaking hand, he grabbed a fistful of my shirt and pulled me up so I was lying over him, and he kissed me.

He was still shaking and his breaths were short and ragged, but my God how he kissed me. Soft, soft kisses, adoring kisses. There was no laughing between us, just half-opened eyes and ragged breaths. Then he rolled us to our sides and wrapped his arms around me, and as he kissed me, his fingers traced the side of my face. It was more intimate than anything we'd done.

His kisses eventually slowed, as did his breathing, the sound a slow metronome lulling me to sleep with him.

When I woke up, I was all snuggled and warm, but the blankets were stuck, so I pulled them as I rolled over. There was a loud thump and a groan, and there was suddenly a lot more room in my bed, which was odd. I looked over to find Levi's bed empty and Levi in a heap on the floor. He looked up at me, not really understanding what just happened. When I laughed at his expression, his mouth fell open. "Did you just push me out of bed?"

I laughed some more and kind of fibbed. "You fell."

He pretended to be put out, but he started to chuckle. "Nice Harrison, real nice."

I held the blankets up for him as a peace offering, and he jumped up and climbed back into bed with me. He faced the front, his back to me, snuggling into me, and he grabbed my arm and curled it around him. "If I'm hitting the floor this time, you're coming with me," he said. We both smiled as we dozed.

THINGS WERE different between us from then on. Our first blowjobs and sleeping in the same bed set a precedent to how we spent the rest of that week.

School time was fine—we went to class, just like normal, we hung out, we studied, we talked and laughed.

But when the doors were closed, it was very different. Sure, we still did our homework and studied, but we made out, we kissed and groped, rubbed and pulled, licked and sucked. We practised our oral skills; I was getting better at it, taking him deeper every time—though I had yet to swallow. Sometimes we'd just hold hands and watch movies on my laptop, but unlike that first time, we always slept in our own beds.

If I had to classify whatever he was to me, it'd be boyfriend.

But I couldn't classify it. I couldn't label him to anyone, because I couldn't tell anyone. And it wasn't like I had to explain this to Levi; he just understood.

Carson seemed content to avoid us, which was fine by me. And by the time Levi had been here for over six weeks, I'd barely given Carson Sinclair a thought.

Though Levi seemed to notice him. "He stares at you," Levi told me. "He's always looking at you."

I told him he was delusional, but he shook his head at me. "I wish you'd see yourself how I see you."

I snorted. "What? My come face?"

Levi laughed and shook his head again. "You know, he would take you back," he stated, matter-of-factly. "If you wanted him, you could have him."

My gaze shot to look at him. "But I don't want him. I told you that. I wouldn't care if he begged me."

"Harrison," he said softly. "I won't be here forever."

His words made my heart squeeze. "I know you're leaving," I told him, angrier than I should have been. "I know you're only here for three months, and I know it's already been six weeks. I know this. I don't need reminding."

"Hey," he put his hands up defensively. He walked over to my bed and sat in front of me. "I don't like the idea of it either," he said quietly. "I wish we had longer too."

I couldn't look at him, but I nodded.

He crawled into my lap, straddling me, and held my face. He kissed my cheek. "I wish we had forever."

"I do too," I whispered.

He kissed me softly, sweetly, and settled himself against me.

That night, he slept in my bed.

CHAPTER 5

THE NEXT WEEKEND I took him to the Art Gallery of New South Wales, and we went to the open-air theatre in the Domain. I tried to take him to everything I thought he should see, all the sights of Sydney, but he was quite content to look at the inner-city buildings.

He pointed out the older, colonial buildings, the churches, and the federation sandstone styles, but he was equally enthralled by the contemporary lines of steel and glass.

"You are so ready to be an architect," I teased him, rolling my eyes.

He laughed and pushed me. "Shut up. It's an *architectural genius* anyway, Doctor Haddon."

His words stopped me, and my smile faded. I groaned. "Don't remind me."

He was quiet beside me for a long while before he sighed. "I wish you'd tell your dad," he said quietly.

"You don't think I've tried?"

"I know you have," he said, clearly frustrated. "Wrong word choice. Sorry. I wish he'd understand. I just wish you didn't have to settle for being miserable to make him happy." Levi frowned and shook his head. "As your father, he should see that!"

"Yeah well, he's not exactly the fatherly type," I mumbled. "He doesn't know me at all."

Levi didn't push it after that. Our mood had taken a nosedive, thanks to me. Seeming to know I needed the distraction, we walked for a while and he pointed out a different building type, marvelling at the structure before him.

I envied his passion. But above all, I envied that he was allowed to follow his heart. I envied that he had no one telling him his dreams weren't good enough or that he would do as he was told, rather than what he wanted.

I envied that he was free to be himself.

———

ON TUESDAY AT SCHOOL, I had music Studio 1 to practise the piano by myself. I needed to get my practical down before my finals, and Father Phillip graciously allowed me to use the room as I pleased.

I hardly needed his guidance. Even he admitted I was a better pianist than him, and he'd been playing for fifty years.

I got lost in my music. I always had. Especially Mozart.

I didn't hear the door open and I didn't see someone step into the room. Only when the Concerto no. 9 was finished did I become aware of being watched.

I turned to find Levi. He was standing against the door. His eyes were wide, but he didn't say a word. I turned back to the keys and opened my mouth to say something, anything, but when I looked back at him again, he was standing behind me.

Slowly, he sat on the edge of my seat, right beside me, and whispered, "Play for me."

So I did.

But I didn't play Mozart or even Beethoven.

I played him my song.

It was nameless. It was melodic and sweet, and something I'd worked on with him in mind. Each note captured the butterflies I got when I saw him, the warmth in my chest when he kissed me, the fleeting, most perfect high in the world.

He was looking at me like I was a puzzle to be solved, like he couldn't believe the music was coming from my hands. When in actual fact, it wasn't coming from my hands at all. It was coming from my heart. And when the last notes of the song held in the air, he shook his head. His eyes were filled with unshed tears, and he whispered, "Harrison... holy shit!"

My heart was hammering. "Didn't you like it?"

He blinked. "Harrison, you have to play."

I looked at him, unsure. "Play what?"

"Just play, Harrison. Forget being a doctor. The world needs to hear you play." I laughed off my embarrassment and his eyes narrowed. "I'm being serious," he said a little loudly in the acoustic room. He quietened down, "Harrison, I've never heard anything like that." He shook his head. "You have a gift."

I told him quietly, "Yeah well, my father doesn't think so."

"Fuck your father!" he snapped, and I blinked back my surprise at his tone. He huffed out a breath, "Sorry. Sorry. I just... it just kills me that you'll give up on your dreams so easily."

I looked at him, but I had no comeback. Because underneath it all, I knew he was right.

"What about you, Harrison?" he asked me. "What about what *you* want?"

I looked down at my hands. I tried to say something; my mouth opened to say something... anything. But I couldn't. Instead, I told him, "I have to go to class."

I got up and left him sitting at the piano.

AFTER SCHOOL when I walked into our room, I barely had the door closed behind me, and Levi was in front of me.

"I'm sorry, I'm sorry," he said. "I didn't mean to upset you." He put his hand on my arm and when I didn't move it away, he slid his hand up to cup my face. "Please tell me we're okay."

I closed my eyes and leaned into his hand. I whispered, "We're okay."

He sighed with relief and pulled me into his arms. "I'm sorry. I didn't mean to push. I know it's not what you want."

"It just upsets me."

"I know, and I'm sorry," he apologized again.

"No, it's not that. It upsets me... because I know you're right."

He didn't reply. He just held me tighter.

"What were you doing, anyway?" I asked him, pulling out of his embrace. "In A block. Biology is in C block."

He grinned. "I've already done the cellular structure of aquatic hyphomycetes. So Father Sedative asked me to take a folder to the Office."

I couldn't help but smile. "Father Sedative?"

"Yeah, he could put anyone to sleep," he said. "Anyway I was walking down the hall when I heard someone banging on the old ivories," he said, rolling his eyes.

I laughed. "Oh, were they any good?"

He looked at me, serious yet still smiling. "It was the sweetest music I've ever heard."

I blushed at his compliment and it made him smile. He pulled me in closer and touched my heated cheek. "Promise you'll play for me again."

I nodded as I pressed my lips to his.

A loud knock at the door scared the crap out of both of us, making us jump apart. Levi covered his mouth with his hand and walked over to his bed, picking up his bag as I opened the door.

"Harrison." Father Collin smiled at me, then looked over my shoulder. He clearly wasn't here to see me. "Levi?"

"Yes, Father?"

"In two weeks' time, the weekend is a four-day boarders' leave weekend, though you should know you're more than welcome to stay. The campus will remain open."

Shit. Four days.

Four days without him.

I couldn't do four days without him.

"Oh, Father," I said quickly. "I've already asked my parents if Levi could come home with me."

Levi caught on, thankfully, and when Father Collin looked at him, he nodded.

"I presume it was fine, then?" he asked.

"Oh, yes. No problems."

"Very well. And Harrison?"

"Yes, Father?"

"Say hello to your father for me," he said with what I thought was supposed to be a smile.

"Shall do."

When Father Collin left, I shut the door and fell backwards onto my bed with a groan. "Shit, that was close."

Levi jumped on me, laughing. "Man, you just lied to a priest!"

I couldn't help but laugh. "Yeah, I'm going to hell."

He leaned down and kissed me with smiling lips. "So, four days with your folks, huh?"

"Yeah well," I shrugged. "What would you prefer? Four days with me or four days with old Father Jabba the Hut and Father Sedative?"

He laughed. "Now you're really going to hell, for calling a priest an overgrown alien slug *and* for lying."

I sat up quickly and flipped him over, so I was lying on him. I grinned and told him, "What I will be going to hell for is what I plan on doing to you tonight."

He groaned and laughed. "I'm only too happy to oblige."

That night when the dorm was dark and quiet, I took his engorged cock in my mouth. And when his body told me he was close to coming, I didn't pull away. I gripped his hips, sucked even harder, and swallowed everything he gave me.

THE TWO WEEKS leading up to our four-day weekend were busy. We did our homework, we fooled around, we went to class, we did laps in the pool, we studied, and we fooled around some more.

Once I'd tasted him, I was never not-swallowing again. And it surprised me to learn that I liked it.

Really, *really* liked it.

There was something about having his cock in my mouth and giving him pleasure that thrilled me. And when his load would coat my throat, as his fingers gripped my hair, it gave me a surge of pride. And pleasure.

Almost as much pleasure as when he did it to me.

And because it was like a drug, once we started really getting into it—trying new positions for blowjobs—we didn't want to stop. Which was the reason why, when my mum came to pick us up, we were both tired and yawning. "Studying hard, boys?" Mum said after we'd yawned through introductions.

"Yeah, Mum." I nodded. "Trial exams when we get back."

Well, it's not as though I could tell her the truth. *No, Mum. Actually giving and receiving head all night for hours and hours on end takes a lot out of you. Though we are really improving; I can open my throat now. His cock just slides right in—*

"Harrison?"

"Huh?" I said, startled out of my filthy daydream.

Mum was obviously repeating herself. "I said, I thought we could spend the days off up at the farm."

"Okay," I agreed. "It'll be good for Levi to see the country."

"Do you guys have a farm?" he asked, wide eyed.

I smiled at him. "It's not really a farm. Not a working farm anyway. It's just a weekender on a couple of acres, that's all."

"Oh," he said, surprised. "Where is it?"

"In the Blue Mountains," Mum answered.

"About two hours from here," I explained.

Mum looked at me. "Your father's arranged some days off. He'll meet us up there tonight."

Oh. Great.

We picked up Holly, who was none too pleased about spending time with the family, or more to the point, spending time away from the new boyfriend.

I couldn't help but smile. I was bringing mine with me.

I gave Holly the front seat, settled in next to said-boyfriend, and we were both asleep before we hit the freeway.

I WOKE up at the turn off to Little Hartley. It was a small town in the heart of the Blue Mountains, my parents' farm was about ten minutes off the main road, and I woke Levi up as we pulled up at the house.

It was getting dark and bitterly cold, and after we'd unpacked our bags, while Mum stocked the pantry, Levi started the wood fire. Holly on the other hand, dressed in black from head to toe, sulked and sighed dramatically.

The Goth phase and "oh how the world hates me" phase suited her.

After we'd had dinner and Mum had asked her usual 'How's school going?' questions, we saw the headlights of my father's car come down the drive. He walked in and kissed his wife, barely acknowledging his two kids. It wasn't surprising, considering he barely knew us.

He smiled kindly at Levi, asking a few questions about his time here in Australia, as we sat around the table. And of course the "I'll see if you're worth your salt" question, "So Levi, what is it you want to do with your life?"

Levi talked animatedly about his love of architecture and engineering. It wasn't that he was trying to impress my father; it was that he was just passionate about it, and it showed.

My father smiled politely. "It's great to see you're so driven for your career," he said, sipping his wine. "Harrison here could learn a thing a two about that."

"Dad—"

"It's one thing to be a doctor, Harrison," he said dismissively. "But it's another thing entirely to be the best."

This would normally be the part where I told him I didn't want to be a doctor, and this was the part where he told me the definition of aspirations and disappointment. But I just didn't have it in me. Not tonight, not in front of Levi.

Even I could hear the defeat in my voice. "Yes, Dad."

My father smiled. "What? No arguments about childhood dreams about playing the piano?"

"Not tonight, no," I said quietly. My father smiled his victory smile, and sitting in front of my parents—the people who were supposed to love me unconditionally—another little part of me died. Mum started talking about her latest fund-raising efforts, but I didn't pay any attention.

I looked over at Levi, and his jaw was clenched so tight it was bulging. His eyes were hard, and he was staring at my father. When he looked over at me, I shook my head.

"Pardon me," he said. "I'm tired, so if I may be excused...?"

"Of course, dear," my mother said with a smile. Then she looked at me and grinned. "Such nice manners."

I tried to smile for her. "I'm going to bed too," I said, not waiting for another word. I followed Levi down the hall, and when I walked into the bedroom, he turned to face me.

He pulled at his hair and whispered, "I'm sorry, Harrison. But he's an arsehole."

I nodded. "Told ya."

He shook his head. "You know what? Ugh," he groaned. "It doesn't matter. I shouldn't say anything, I know it only makes you feel bad."

I shrugged. "I'm used to him. Don't let him get to you."

"Harrison," he said my name as he grabbed me by the tops of my arms. His eyes were wide and urgent. "You need to stand up to him. You need to tell him to go to fucking hell."

I snorted. "I thought you weren't going to say anything?"

He sighed, exasperated, frustrated. He pointed to the door, to where my father was. "How can that not bother you?"

"Because I've had eighteen years to get used to it," I told him.

He was so worked up, so angry, he couldn't even form words. He was pacing and pulling at his hair. I grabbed his arm with one hand and his face with my other, and I kissed him.

After a moment, he pulled away. "Kissing me won't distract me," he whispered with a smile, but the fight was gone from his voice.

"Then I didn't kiss you properly enough," I whispered, and when I was done kissing him, he wasn't angry anymore.

———

THE NEXT MORNING AT BREAKFAST, I told Mum I thought it'd be a good idea for Levi to see the sights. I suggested we could drive into town and do the tourist thing for the said English tourist just as Dad walked in with his phone to his ear. He was talking surgery or something, and Mum looked at me and smiled apologetically. These types of phone calls usually ended with, "Okay, I'm on my way."

I sighed and imitated my father's voice, "Okay, I'm on my way," two seconds before my father said it.

He had to leave. Of course he did. But then Mum started making arrangements for us all to pack up and go back to Sydney.

"What? We just got here," I complained. "Levi can't say he went to the Blue Mountains and saw none of it."

Mum looked at me, then Levi, then back to me. "Can you two be trusted to look after the place on your own?"

"Mum, I'm eighteen," I replied. "And I've been looking after myself at school for the last six years. I'm sure I'll be fine."

She scowled at me as Dad yelled something from the bedroom about knowing coming here was a bad idea and leaving in five minutes. Holly already had her phone to her ear, squealing she'd be back in town in two hours, as she packed with her free hand.

Exactly five minutes later, Mum was telling me to not let the fire go out, make sure we eat something other than junk food, and to drive her car carefully—she expected it back without a scratch by midday Monday—while Dad was waiting impatiently in his car. Holly was smiling for the first time since we picked her up yesterday, and Mum was still giving me directives through the window as the car sped down the drive.

I closed the front door and Levi, sitting on a kitchen stool, blinked and grinned. "What the hell just happened?"

"We have the entire house to ourselves for three days, that's what just happened."

"Man, I gotta say," he said shaking his head "your family is weird."

I walked over to him, pushing myself between his open legs. "Promise me you won't talk about my family for the next three days." I pecked his lips and smiled. "We have the entire house to ourselves for three days," I repeated. "I don't want to think about anyone but you and me."

He hummed. "So, what do you wanna do first?" he asked and waggled his eyebrows.

"Well, I thought we could do the sightseeing thing today."

His eyes widened. "Oh. Seriously?"

I laughed at the disappointment in his voice. "Well, we should go into town and pick up a few things," I told him. "We can have a look around." Then I added, "There'll be plenty of time for *other things*. Three days' worth of time."

He grinned and kissed me but reluctantly agreed. So we got dressed and made the drive into Little Hartley. There were boutique shops and cafés, but I drove him around and we did the tourist thing, even doing a smaller trail walk. The Blue Mountains were famous for a reason: they were stunning. Australian flora and fauna were putting on their winter show. There was no snow here this winter, but it was still bitterly cold, and the fresh air tinged with eucalyptus was great for the soul.

When our stomachs growled, we headed back into town and grabbed some lunch. We called into the supermarket to pick up a three-day supply of junk food, bread and milk, and when Levi spied a coffee shop, I suggested he go in and order.

I quickly dashed into the pharmacy, and before Levi had come back out with two coffees, I had my purchase hidden in my inside jacket pocket.

We drove back to the house, unloaded the groceries, packed them away, and then I added some logs to the fire. And while Levi freshened up, I had an idea. I tried to lift the queen-sized mattress off the bed in our room, but it was too heavy. "Levi, can you help me here?" I yelled.

"Jesus," he said when he saw what I was doing. He grabbed the other corner and helped me drag it out to the lounge room. We pushed the lounges back, making room, and when the mattress was down in front of the fire, Levi flopped down on it and asked, "Can I ask why you wanted this out here?"

"'Cause this is where we're gonna sleep," I told him, like he didn't already know. "In front of the fire."

And I was suddenly very nervous.

I was about to ask him to take my virginity and ask for his in return. Well, his boy-sex virginity.

"Aawww, such a romantic," he said, grinning.

I laughed, giving my nerves away, and Levi noticed. He eyed me curiously.

I knelt on the mattress and leaned over him. He cupped my face, his eyes searching mine. "Harrison, what's up?"

"Um." My mouth was suddenly very dry. I tried to swallow. "I want... I thought...."

He smirked at my inability to speak and rolled us over, so he was now on top of me. "Just say it, Harrison."

"I want to give you something," I told him.

His eyes lit up. "I love surprises! And presents!"

I chuckled at him.

"What is it? *Where* is it?" he asked excitedly.

I laughed nervously. "Um, me," I answered quietly. "I want to give myself to you."

It only took him a second to get it. His eyes went wide. "Harrison...."

Oh, shit. He didn't want to.

Not that he didn't want to have sex. He didn't want me. Cold dread and rejection lumped in my gut. "It's okay if you don't want to," I added quickly. "I just thought—"

And then he was kissing me, very fucking deeply. His hands surrounded my face and he pressed his weight onto me, writhing and grinding himself on me.

But then he pulled away suddenly, as though something just occurred to him. "Ugh. We can't," he said with a disappointed groan. "We don't have anything with us. Like supplies and stuff."

I smiled. "Yes we do. I bought some today."

"Is that why you ditched me at the coffee shop?" he asked with a smile.

I smiled and nodded. "I know you've done this kind of thing before... with a girl. But I haven't, and to be honest I'm fucking petrified, but I want it. I want to do this," I rambled. Then I whispered, "I want you to be the one."

"I've never had, you know, anal sex with a guy before," he said softly. "I don't really know what I'm doing...."

I rolled my eyes. "Exactly how much porn have we watched together?"

He snorted. "A bit."

I slid my hands down and squeezed his arse cheeks, grinding him into my hips. "More than a bit. And we've practically done everything else."

"True," he conceded. Leaning down, he pecked my lips. Then he nodded. "It'd be an honour to be your first."

And in the middle of the afternoon on the floor in front of the fire, I gave myself to him.

We were both young, inexperienced, and anxious; we fumbled a little and laughed nervously as we undressed each other. But we soon found our rhythm. We got back to being *us*—to the familiarity of how we were in bed together, the way we'd made out countless times, the way we'd stroked each other, the way he took me into his mouth. Because this was Levi. The one person who I knew would never hurt me or embarrass me. The one person who made me feel safe, wanted, and good enough. He already had my heart. Giving him my body was the next best thing.

He had me so caught up in the feeling of his warm, wet mouth and the way his other hand was cupping and massaging my balls, I didn't think twice about his fingers rubbing around my arse.

It was only when he pressed his first finger into me that I remembered what we were doing. He must have felt me tense, because he worked my cock harder.

He could read my body, what I liked, what I didn't. And he worked my arse, circling and stretching while he sucked and pumped. When I groaned, he slipped a second slicked finger in.

And I didn't mind the burn, the stretch. In fact, I didn't mind it at all.

I found myself moving with him, rocking and moaning. And he sucked me until I came. I swear he sucked my orgasm right out of me.

And even though the room was still spinning, I could hear the tear of foil. Levi grabbed my legs and pushed my knees up toward my arms—my body was so pliable and boneless, willing and ready.

He leaned over me, bringing his face closer to mine. His eyes were wide and pure, silently asking if I still wanted to do this.

I nodded.

And he did it.

He slowly pushed into me. His eyes were squeezed shut, his mouth was open, and his body trembled.

And it hurt, the intrusion, the breach, the burn, but only a little. The look of him above me, knowing he was inside me—that I was really doing this—was all I needed.

"Not gonna last," he said quickly. He exhaled in a puff and his eyes flew open, and he stared at me. His breath was quiet and quivering, "Ohmygod... holy fuck, Harrison... are you okay?"

"Yeah," I answered breathily. And he pulled out and pushed back into me, making me gasp.

When is eyes flashed to mine, I pulled his face in so I could kiss him. He pushed my knees up higher, and he thrust into me slowly. He was trying to hold back, he was trying not to hurt me.

My mouth found his neck and when I sucked his skin into my mouth, he groaned and grunted, thrusting again before stretching out over me. His body trembled, and I could feel his pulse, his heartbeat, as he surged and came inside me.

He collapsed on me, his weight felt so good. He groaned, mumbling into my neck, words I couldn't understand. Finally, he pulled his hips back, pulling out of me, but quickly settled himself back on me, kissing my neck and shoulder.

"Are you okay?" he asked.

I nodded. "Very okay."

"I'm sorry I didn't last long," he said quietly. "It felt too good."

I pulled his face back, kissing his lips. "It was perfect. You were perfect."

"Really?" he asked, doubtfully.

I nodded. Then he asked, "How's your... um your...?"

"My arse?" I said it for him. He bit his lip and nodded. I wiggled underneath him, and said, "A little sore but otherwise, very fucking good."

"Thank you," he whispered.

I laughed. "Thank you."

"You are so welcome, baby. Two four seven, three six five."

He kissed me then, before rolling off me and cleaning us up. I stretched out in front of the fire, Levi grabbed a blanket, and we fell asleep wrapped around each other.

CHAPTER 6

THE NEXT DAY, the sound of rain and the smell of bacon woke me up. I rolled over and found the fire stoked and roaring, but his side of the mattress was empty. I called out, "The smell of frying bacon better be the reason you're not in here with me."

He laughed. "And eggs. Am I forgiven?"

I leaned up on an elbow and watched him in the kitchen. He was wearing trackies and an old rugby shirt of mine, as he wrestled with the fry pan. He was fucking gorgeous.

"What are you smiling at?" he asked, catching me staring.

"Just my very own sexy, personal chef."

"Oh, har har," he said. "Now get your sexy arse outta bed."

I was still naked, and knowing we had the house completely to ourselves, I got up, took a few steps, and stretched.

Levi groaned, the pan forgotten, as I scratched my arse and walked to the bathroom with a grin.

When I was dressed, he had breakfast plated up, and before I sat down beside him, I pulled his chin up and kissed him. He grinned shyly as he started to eat.

I chuckled at him and took a mouthful of scrambled eggs.

And I fucking groaned.

Which of course, made him groan.

I laughed at him and swallowed my food. "I'm starving," I said with my mouth half full. "And this is really good."

He beamed. "Thanks."

"So what do you want to do today?"

He motioned toward the mattress. "I'd like to not venture too far from right there."

"Don't you wanna see the sights?"

He shook his head slowly. "Hm mm." He pointed his thumb to the rain-spattered window. "Perfect weather to stay indoors," he said with half a smirk.

So that was exactly what we did.

All day; we made out in the kitchen, gave hand jobs in the shower, laid all over each other watching movies, made out on the lounge... all the things we could never do at school.

When we'd cleaned up after dinner, we fell back onto the mattress. Levi pulled me over him, so I was snug between his legs. His eyes roamed my face, and he shook his head, like he couldn't believe his own thoughts.

"Levi?" I prompted him to speak his mind.

"I never thought I'd want to," he said. "To be honest, I don't think I'll like it, but I'd like to try."

I pecked his lips. "What are you talking about?"

"I want *you* to top *me*," he said quietly. "I want to bottom for you."

Holy shit. I knew he'd said before the thought of

bottoming scared him, but I could understand his curiosity. I pulled back so I could see his face clearly. "Are you sure?" I asked him.

He nodded, but he looked a little scared. "Will you stop if I ask you to?"

"Of course," I told him. "Of course I would."

But he didn't ask me to stop. Even when I'd stretched him like they do in the porn we'd watched, and like he did to me, he didn't ask me to stop. I sucked him so hard his back left the mattress as he came in my mouth. I rolled on a condom and slicked us up some more, and when I pushed the head of my dick into him, he gasped and moaned, but he didn't ask me to stop.

It was so goddamn tight, and hot, and really fucking good. But he looked uncomfortable, like I was hurting him. "Want me to stop?" I asked in quick huffs.

He shook his head. "No. Don't stop," he whispered. "Keep going."

I pushed slowly, slowly, until I was buried inside him. It wasn't like anything else in the world. And the pressure in my belly and at the base of my spine took flight, and I couldn't stop it. It was too hot, too much, too good, and when Levi groaned underneath me, I came.

When my senses came back to me, he was kissing my face, my eyelids, and whispering something about *beautiful*.

And later, when we finally fell asleep, it was with my arms wrapped around him. But when we woke, I was cocooned into his side and enveloped in his arms.

And I never wanted to move.

The next two days were exactly the same. Totally absorbed in each other, making out, making love. Though I admitted to him that I preferred to bottom—I didn't know why, I just did. I liked being taken care of. I liked the feeling of him possessing me, of being his.

And when we woke up on Monday, it was with heavy hearts that we packed up, put our bags into the car, and locked the house.

We spent three wonderful days oblivious to the outside world. "I don't want to go back," he said as we got into the car. "I wish there was some way for us to be together."

"We're together at school," I offered weakly.

He sighed. "No. I mean together for real."

"I know," I agreed quietly. "I don't want to have to deal with exams and my father." Then I leaned in and kissed him softly. "I don't want to have to deal with you leaving. So if you can think of a way, please let me know."

BACK AT SCHOOL, things were as they always were, but also very different.

School was the same, though most of our classes were spent studying. Oh, and I was no longer a virgin, though no one else could tell.

Or that I was in love.

I'd fallen for him. I was *in love* with him.

And he was leaving in two weeks.

It was with this bittersweet ache in my chest that I performed my practical music exam. The joy of finding love and the accompanying pain of losing him echoed through my fingers to the piano.

I bared my soul and my heavy heart right there in front of everyone. I got so lost in my music. It was an extension of who I was. The special exam adjudicators seemed happy with my performance, and Father Collin later told me he'd never seen me play so beautifully.

Whether it was nerves or if I was just lost in my music, I had no idea Levi had snuck in to watch me perform. And I had no idea he recorded it on my phone. When I went back to our room, he was lying on my bed with his laptop and my phone. "What are you doing?" I asked him.

"Promise you won't get mad."

Well, that was ominous. I walked over and plonked myself down beside him. I was relieved my exam was over. The stress was a weight off my mind. It was then I looked at what Levi was doing. He was completing a form of some description, and it took me a moment to read it and figure out the meaning.

He was completing an application to the Royal Academy of Music.

A music degree.

In London.

For me.

It took a few goes for my voice to work right. "Wh—wh —what are you doing?"

"You said to find a way that we can be together for real," he said quickly. "You said if I could find a way, to let you know. Well, this is it."

I told him, like I'd told him a hundred times, "I can't study music, Levi! I'm supposed to be going to medical school in Sydney. Not a music school in London! What were you thinking?"

"Look at this," he said quietly. "Look at this and tell me this isn't what you should be doing," he said and pressed play on my phone.

And he had captured me, at the piano. I was lost in the music, coaxing the piano to sing my haunted lullaby. "Do you see what I see?" he asked, with tears in his eyes. "Do you see how I see you?" He took my hand and placed it over his heart. "Do you feel what I feel?"

My hand fisted his shirt and I nodded. "Yes, I feel what you feel."

"Then don't throw your dreams away like they don't matter," he said, and his tears spilled down his cheeks. "Because they *do* matter."

"Levi—"

He grabbed my face, my jaw, and rested his forehead against mine. "Please Harrison, don't say goodbye."

I kissed him then, and we fell back onto the bed. And that night, for hours, we made love. That was what it was. Love. Slow, unhurried, savouring love.

And when he was sound asleep, I started up my laptop, completed the half done application, and hit submit.

FOR THE NEXT TWO WEEKS, Levi's last two weeks, his impending departure lumped in my chest. He was adamant he wouldn't be saying goodbye—not now, not ever, he said. We just found each other, he told me, and now that I'd submitted my application for the Royal Academy, it was a done deal.

He was so fucking cocky and sure of himself, sure I'd get accepted, sure of us.

But when I asked him how the hell I was supposed to tell my father, he had no answer.

"Tell him while I'm here," he said. "You need all the support you can get, and I'll be here to hold your hand."

"You want to hold my hand in front of my father?"

He snorted. "You know what I mean."

"I'm not telling him anything until I'm sure I've got a spot at the Academy. It's my one chance. If they say no, then I can say I tried."

Levi's jaw bulged. "One chance? That's bollocks Harrison and you know it."

"Bollocks?"

"Shut up."

We both kind of laughed, and I took a deep breath. "I don't want to fight with you, Levi. I don't want to fight with my dad either."

"I get that, I really do. I just want to be here for you when you tell him."

I shook my head. "Because I know, I just know if I told him now, he'd find a way to cancel my application."

Levi's eyes went wide. "He wouldn't."

I shrugged. "Wouldn't he?"

"There are other schools," Levi said defiantly. "And if he cancels that application, we'll just apply somewhere else."

I kissed him quiet. "Thank you. Thank you for... everything. I wish I could find out right now, I wish I knew now so I could tell my father. But we'll just have to wait."

And that was the irony of time.

I needed time to hurry up—so I could hear back about my application—and I needed to stop time all together. Because Levi was leaving and I was running out of fucking days.

Every minute that passed, I was one minute closer to knowing about my future and one minute closer to losing him.

And two weeks... well, two weeks both dragged and flew.

I walked into our room and threw my books onto my

desk. "I still haven't heard anything," I whined in a huff. Levi didn't say anything, so I looked over at him.

And he was packing his bag.

"What are you doing?" I asked, even though it was pretty fucking obvious.

"Harrison," he said quietly. "I leave in the morning."

I shook my head. "No. We've got another week, or a few days, or something...."

His eyes fell. "I wish that were true."

I shook my head again. "No."

"Please don't make it any harder than it is already," he said. "And don't act like we're never going to see each other again. Because we will."

"Levi—"

"Remember my promise to you. Two four seven, three six five."

He was always so sure, so confident. He said it like he knew it.

I nodded, but I was not convinced.

And that night when we climbed into bed, what started out like our usual gentle, rhythmic lovemaking soon turned urgent, hard, and primal. I was laying face down and he was over me, between my legs, pounding into me.

Like he knew exactly what I needed.

His fingers were digging into me, his cock was buried inside me, and he thrust roughly, deeply.

Beautifully.

"Shh," he whispered into my shoulder, and I realized I was moaning loudly. But I didn't care. Then he stopped abruptly, still inside me, his forehead rested on my shoulder. "God, I'm hurting you...."

"Don't stop," I demanded him, lifting my arse. "Don't fucking stop. I want to feel you for days." I raised my hips, offering more of me to him. "Please, please. Fuck me, please."

One hand gripped my hip, his other hand gripped my shoulder, and he fucked me. For all he was worth. Oh, God... it was so fucking good.

He impaled me, so completely, and pushed harder into me. I could feel him swell as he fell forward, and his cock erupted in short bursts into the condom. And when he collapsed on top of me, he sobbed. I turned underneath him, wrapped my arms around him, and held him.

And we slept.

CHAPTER 7

WHEN I WOKE up a few hours later, he had me in his mouth. "Jesus."

"I want to taste you," he said as he licked me. "I want to remember how you taste on my tongue."

It didn't take long until I was gripping the sheets beside us as he took my load into his throat.

We stayed awake, refusing to miss another minute, and as the sun turned Levi's face from moonlight-silver to daylight-flush, he pushed inside me once more. He was gentle, took his time, kissing my mouth, my neck, my eyelids. He held my face and whispered how he loved me, how he couldn't imagine life without me. He murmured how lucky he was to have found his soul mate at eighteen, and how this wasn't goodbye.

"This is just the beginning," he murmured against my ear as he slowly thrust into me. "It's not goodbye. I love you, Harrison. We're just starting. This is just the beginning."

His words made me cry, and he held me so much tighter. He kissed me so much deeper, and I could feel the honesty in his words. I could feel how much he loved me.

It wasn't goodbye.

It was just the beginning.

And as we got to the departure gates, he said it again. "This is not goodbye," he said quietly, so Miss Goff didn't hear.

He'd said goodbye to everyone else at school, only Miss Goff and I had come to see him leave. We put it off for as long as we could, but they inevitably announced final boarding call.

If this isn't a goodbye, why does it feel like it is?

Why does it hurt, so fucking much?

And when they told him he had to walk out of my life, I didn't care if people saw. I didn't care if Miss Goff was standing right fucking there. I grabbed him and threw my arms around him. I kissed his neck and he gripped onto me, holding me so damn tight. "I think you've just aged Miss Goff ten years," he mumbled into my neck.

I pulled back, just a little. "I don't care." I kissed him, right there in front of two smiling check-in clerks and one very wide-eyed teacher.

Levi threw his head back and laughed and grinned all the way through the boarding gate.

I waited until I couldn't see him anymore, then waited until Miss Goff put her hand on my arm. "You okay?" she asked.

"No," I croaked, shaking my head as my tears spilled down my cheeks.

"Come on," she said softly, leading us toward the exit.

Stunned into silence, Miss Goff clearly wasn't going to bring it up, so I waited until we'd driven some distance before I asked, "Do you have to tell the school... you know, about what you saw... about me and Levi?"

"No," she said, looking from the road to me. "Firstly,

Levi was technically not a student at the time, and secondly, it's none of the school's business."

I almost cried again. "Thank you," I said sincerely.

"Do your parents know?" she asked me gently.

I barked out a laugh. "Um, no. My father is disappointed enough with me."

"Oh, Harrison," she said softly. But she said nothing else. There was nothing else really she could say.

I looked at her. "I don't want to be a doctor."

"I know," she said.

"I've applied to enrol at a music school," I told her. Her eyes went wide as she drove, so I figured I may as well divulge all. "In London. With Levi." Just saying it made my chest warm. "An application for a bachelor's degree, actually."

She looked at me, then back to the road, then back to me. Then she laughed. "Good for you, Harrison," she said with the biggest grin. "You have no idea how happy I am to hear that."

I smiled. "Really? Because my father is going to shit bricks." And then I remembered I was talking to a teacher. "Sorry."

"It's okay, Harrison," she smiled. "Your father may very well... *pass masonry...* but it's your life. Not his."

Pass masonry. I snorted.

"Let me know if there's anything I can do to help, okay?" she asked. "You should follow your heart."

"Yeah well," I admitted. "My heart just boarded a plane for England."

She looked at me and smiled sadly. "I saw."

We pulled up at school and Miss Goff told me to head straight to my room, she'd have me excused from study group. But my room wasn't the same anymore. It was empty. I fell onto his bed, closed my eyes, ignored my broken heart, and slept.

THE DAYS BLURRED into each other after that. My other exams were approaching, and my time was spent between studying and Skyping with Levi.

We talked every day, usually my mornings, which were his evenings, and sometimes I'd log on in the middle of the night, just to hear his voice.

And two weeks after Levi left, I got called to Admin. I all but ran to the office, hoping it was news of my application. But the anticipation and hope were pretty short lived when I got led into an office and found my father and mother sitting there, stone-faced, unhappy, disappointed.

Father Collin was there, and so was Miss Goff. I started to panic when I realized what this could be about. This wasn't about my application. I'd been found out—my father knew I was gay. Miss Goff seemed to understand from the look of sheer dread on my face, because she was the first to explain. "Harrison, the school has received a formal request for a reference for London's Royal Academy of Music."

I sighed in relief. "Wait, what?" I asked. "They want a reference?"

"It's protocol for the school to contact the parents before such information is divulged," Father Collin went on to say.

I looked at my father, and he said with a biting tone, "Only we didn't know anything about a *music* application. Did we, Harrison?"

I didn't answer. I tried to swallow down my heart—it was in my throat making it impossible to breathe. I looked to Miss Goff, but Father Collin spoke instead. "St Michael's can't give a reference with good conscience, knowing your father objects."

So that was what it comes down to. Who fucking pays. My mind was scrambling, clutching at the few straws of hope I had left. "Father Collin, how much are the annual school fees?" I asked.

My question seemed to surprise him. "Why?"

"Because I'm eighteen. And if I pay my own school fees, then my father has nothing to do with my being here. He has no bearing on my attendance, no bearing on the school's responsibility to me."

"How do you expect to pay that amount of money on your own?" Father Collin asked.

"I have my grandmother's trust fund. I'm over eighteen. I can spend it however I want. And if that's to pay school fees, so be it." I had intended on using that money to live off for the next four years in London, but if I had to use it now, I would.

My father looked at me, very surprised. "Harrison, I think we can discuss this at home."

I looked around the office. "This school is my home."

"Harrison—"

"No, Dad. You're not listening. I don't want to be a doctor. It's great that you found your calling, saving people's lives, holding their hearts in your hands. But that's your dream, not mine."

Just then, his mobile phone rang. He groaned at the timing but took the call. My father started, "Can this wait? I'm in the middle of something."

I laughed.

"Harrison, please," my mother admonished me. "His job is very important."

"Yes, it is," I agreed quietly. "But so am I." It wasn't something I had ever believed, until I'd met Levi.

The person on the other end of the phone's voice was buzzing and I looked at Father Collin and Miss Goff. This proved my fucking point. Miss Goff smiled sadly at me, and I shook my head at her and whispered, "Okay, I'm on my way."

Two seconds later, my father said the exact same thing. *Okay, I'm on my way.*

I laughed again.

"Something amuse you, Harrison?" My father asked, closing his phone.

I snorted. "Not at all."

"I have to go," he declared standing up. "But this is far from over."

I stood up too. "Yes, it is."

"Harrison, you're not throwing your life away on some flippant whim to play the damn piano."

"Doctor Haddon," Miss Goff said, now standing beside me. "With all due respect, sir, it's hardly a flippant whim. Harrison is very talented." My father stared at her but she held his gaze. "Have you ever heard him play?"

I snorted. "Of course he hasn't."

My father looked at me, then at Miss Goff. "Well, no... I'm a busy man."

"I'll be writing the reference, Doctor Haddon," she said, dismissively. "With or without Board approval. Harrison deserves the opportunity. He deserves to be heard."

Frustrated, my father looked from Father Collin to his watch. "I have to go," he said, walking toward the door, my mother followed him dutifully.

"That's right. My father, the great cardiologist," I said

sourly. "You're so concerned about everyone else's hearts. What about mine?"

He looked at me then, seemingly lost for words. "Harrison... I...." Then he added quietly, "That's not fair."

"No," I agreed. "It never has been."

And when his phone rang again, he sighed. Pulling it from his pocket, he looked at me, then at his phone.

"Take the call, Dad," I told him. "You certainly don't want to disappoint anyone."

With an exasperated sigh, he put the phone to his ear, and I didn't even watch him leave.

I turned back to Miss Goff. "Thank you," I told her sincerely. "I appreciate what you've done for me. But I don't expect you to jeopardise your job at the school—"

"Harrison," she cut me off with a smile. "It's my job as careers advisor is to help the students, not the parents." She turned to Father Collin. "Isn't that right, Father?"

He gave us a rather dramatic sigh, but then he nodded. "Yes, that's right."

Miss Goff looked at me and grinned. "Go back to your studies, then come and see me after lunch."

I ran to my room. But I didn't look at the books on my bed, I flipped open my laptop and hit Skype. I tapped my fingers impatiently, praying Levi was somewhere near his computer. "Come on, come on, come on, come on...."

"Hey, shouldn't you be in class?"

I grinned at the sound of his voice, his accent, then as his face appeared on my screen.

"Levi, you're not gonna believe what happened!"

"What?"

"The Royal Academy of Music emailed the school. They want a reference!" I told him in a rush. I explained how they phoned my parents, and when they knew nothing of it, they both came in. I told Levi how I told my father, for the final time, I'm not cut out to be a doctor and how I'd pay my own school fees so he has no say in the school's response for the reference. "Miss Goff told my dad she's writing it whether he likes it or not."

His eyes went wide. "Holy fucking shit!"

"Levi Embry Aston!" a female voice called from off-screen. "You will not swear in this house!"

"Embry?" I asked. "What the hell kinda name is that?"

Then Levi was gone from in front of the screen, and I could hear muffled voices, before he came back on screen with a woman in tow.

"Mum, this is Harrison," he said, grinning.

"Mmm, Harrison," she repeated with a nod, as though she'd heard all about me. Her accent seemed thicker than Levi's. She had a round face, but was smiling beautifully. "The boy who's got my son all tied up in knots."

I immediately thought of Levi with his legs bent up near his chest, almost in a knot, and I could feel myself blush. "Um, yeah."

Levi whispered something I couldn't hear, and his mum swatted him with her hand. "I didn't mean literally!" she said with a laugh. "I meant figuratively speaking."

Levi laughed and his mother looked back at me and rolled her eyes. "Nice to finally meet you, Harrison," she said with a smile that matched her son's.

"You'll get to meet him in person soon, Mum," Levi said with a grin. "He's been accepted to the Royal Academy of Music, here in London."

"Well, I haven't been accepted yet—" I tried to explain.

"You will be," he said, looking at me seriously. Then he turned to his Mum. "It's okay if he stays here, isn't it, Mum? He can stay with me, can't he?"

Holy shit. "Jeez, Levi... nice to put her on the spot. Thanks a lot."

She turned back to the screen, looking me up and down. "You look like you need feeding up, love," she said with a nod.

Levi grinned magnificently, and I took it that was a yes.

He kissed her cheek and she smiled at him, mumbled something about boys that need looking after, and disappeared from the screen.

Levi was practically bouncing. "Oh, baby, I can't wait."

Oh, baby.

He called me baby. I grinned. "Neither can I."

He paused. "What did you mean about paying your own school fees?"

"Well, then my father has no say about what college wants what reference."

His jaw bulged and his eyes hardened in what I recognise as his pissed off face. "That's such bollocks, Harrison."

I smiled at his Britishness.

"Just give me the dates you want to leave and I'll take care of the airfare," he said.

"Levi, thank you, but how about we just wait until we hear back from them?"

We didn't have to wait long.

Seven days and two exams later, some random junior kid knocked on my dorm room door telling me I was wanted in Admin.

I raced there, and Miss Goff grinned when she saw me. "I know you've got your final exam tomorrow, and I considered withholding this until it was over so you weren't distracted... but I couldn't." She was just about bubbling over with excitement when she held out a letter from the Royal Academy of Music, addressed to me. "Open it!"

My heart was pounding. This was it. This basically decided if I got to study music, and if I got to see Levi again. I ripped the envelope and pulled out the thick, folded letter.

Dear Mr Haddon,

The Royal Academy of Music is pleased to offer you placement under our international program.

I looked up at Miss Goff and Father Collin, who had since joined in. And I nodded.

And Miss Goff started to laugh with tears in her eyes.

"What exactly did you say in that reference?" I asked her.

She smiled and threw back her hand like it was nothing. "I phoned them, told them your story, explained how you'd used your trust fund money to pay for an expensive school in hopes it would open doors into prestigious music schools," she said with a grin. "Made it sound very dramatic. They were very impressed with your video."

I smiled at her. "I don't know what to say." I shook my head, at a loss for adequate words. "You've helped me like no one else ever has. I could never thank you enough."

Her eyes glistened. "You just did, Harrison. Anyway, you got yourself accepted, not me." Then she smiled and reminded me, "I think there's someone you need to tell."

Levi.

Oh my God.

And the letter in my hand suddenly became very, very real.

I was going to see Levi.

No, scratch that... I was going to *live* with Levi.

In London.

With Levi.

I grinned and nodded and ran like a bat out of hell to my room. I looked at the time. Three here meant six in the morning over there. He should be up. Surely. I started my laptop, hit Skype, and Levi answered almost immediately though I could only see half his sleepy face.

"Oh, hey," he said huskily. "I was just lying in bed thinking about you..."

I grinned. "Levi—"

"...dreaming about you. Having you bent over the back of a sofa." He groaned. "And I've got hold of your hips. I'm fucking you so hard..."

"Levi—" I tried again.

"...fuck, I wish it was real. I tell ya, Harrison, if you were here right now, I'd be inside you."

I swallowed. *Fuck.* "Levi," I mumbled, suddenly out of breath. "In two days you will be."

Silence. "What?"

"I said, in two days you will be," I repeated. "I have an exam tomorrow, but I could leave on the first flight to London straight after." I couldn't stop my grin or the bubble of laughter. "Because my classes at London's Royal Academy of Music start in September."

The screen moved and the sound muffled as though he'd just sat up in bed. When his face appeared on the screen in front of me, he was wide eyed and slack jawed. "Seriously?" he asked. "Don't joke with me, baby. Don't lie to me."

I held the letter in front of my screen with shaking hands so he could see it, and I read it to him.

His hand covered his mouth and his wide eyes shined. I could see a slow smile spread from underneath his fingers. When his hand fell away, he was wearing a full-on grin.

I laughed. "Now, what were you saying before?" I asked, still grinning. "Something about being inside me?"

"Oh, baby," he said with a laugh. "In two days, I'll show you."

MY FINAL EXAM passed in a daze, and I walked back to my dorm room to pack my things. Mum was picking me up from school to take me home for my last night. I was flying out in the morning. I didn't want to waste another minute.

I left my text books on my desk and started packing clothes when there was a knock at my door. "Come in."

The door opened, and when I looked up, it wasn't at all who I expected.

Carson.

"Can I have a word?" he asked quietly.

I threw the shirts I was holding into my suitcase and looked at him. "Sure."

He walked in and closed the door behind him. Taking a deep breath, he wiped his hands on his school pants and looked around nervously. "So, I hear you're going to England."

I smiled, even at the mention of it. "Yeah. To study music."

"You won't be here for graduation?" he asked.

I shook my head. "Nah, my classes start in about two weeks."

He nodded and looked at me. "That's really great, Harrison," he said softly. "And your dad agreed?"

He knew of my struggle with my dad. He had the same problem with his own father. "He didn't have a choice," I explained. "I told him I wasn't going to medical school, that I was eighteen, and he couldn't make me."

He looked at me then. I couldn't be sure, but I think he was... jealous?

"I could never do that," he said quietly, looking away.

"Is being a lawyer something you want?" I asked him.

He shrugged but didn't answer. He looked around my room, at my half-packed suitcases and when he looked back at me, he said, "So whereabouts in England are you going?"

"London."

His eyes went wide as he made the connection. "So you and Levi?"

"Yes. Me and Levi."

He looked at me, really looked at me, and he nodded. He whispered, "Did you come out?"

I barked out a laugh and shook my head. "No. I think my dad can only handle so much disappointment at once."

"But you will one day, won't you," he said. It wasn't a question, it was a statement.

"Yes."

He nodded again. He was being very quiet, very polite, very un-like Carson.

So I asked him to get to his point. "I have a lot of packing to do before my mum gets here," I explained. "Is there something else you wanted?"

"Oh, um," he stammered. "I just wanted to say...." He trailed away.

"Say what, Carson?" I prompted him as I started packing my bags. It was probably a little rude of me, but this guy had made my life hell. I didn't have to worry about him tormenting me anymore.

"I've thought a lot about... what we did," he said, biting his lip. "And how I freaked out. Anyway, I just wanted to say I'm sorry for being a jerk to you this last year, and if I wasn't so gutless, maybe things would have turned out different."

Well, holy shit.

All this time, Levi was right.

I huffed down my nose and gave him a laugh. "You mean if it was something you had wanted, you would have let it happen, regardless of what I wanted. That's what you mean, that if you wanted me, you could have me."

He looked at me, startled.

"Well, Carson," I said, throwing clothes into my suitcase. "Here's the thing, I don't want you. I know who I want, and he's in London. He taught me to follow my heart, unlike you, who made me feel like shit to make yourself feel better."

He opened his mouth a few times, but in the end said a very quiet, "Sorry."

"Don't be," I told him. "I'm not."

The truth was, if Carson hadn't have given Levi a reason to try and make him jealous, maybe we never would have gotten together. I didn't tell Carson that. "Anyway," I changed topics. "I have a lot to get done, so if you don't mind...." I led off suggestively, with a pointed glance at the door.

"Oh, sure." Carson got to the door, and he looked back at me. "Thanks, and good luck."

It should have been enough—such poetic justice—I was getting to live my dream: studying music, not having to hide my sexuality, and Carson would be off to law school under his suffocating father's watchful eye.

But it was somehow kinda hollow. I didn't want him to be miserable. I didn't want anyone to go through what I'd gone through.

"Carson." I stopped him. "Same to you. Good luck, I

mean. And don't be afraid to stand up for yourself. Who knows, you might just be surprised."

He nodded and tried to smile as he walked out, closing the door behind him.

I finished packing up my room, fitting everything into two large suitcases. The room looked bare, and it looked drab and dull. But I couldn't help but smile at my memories of my time here. My memories of the things Levi and I did in here, on that bed, on that desk, even on the chair.

And with a smile, I closed the door for the very last time. I walked the halls of the school that had also been my home for the last six years.

When I got to the front Admin office, my mum was already there. She was talking to Father Collin, and when I walked in, they stopped and looked at me. "You ready?" Mum asked.

I was so fucking ready. Ready to leave, ready to start living my life. "Sure am."

But first things first. "I need to organise payment of my fees," I told them. "I could give you my forwarding address if that's easier."

"No need, Harrison," Father Collin said. "Your dad already took care of it."

That surprised me. A fucking lot. "He what?"

Mum answered. "We weren't ever going to use your money to pay for school fees."

"But he said—"

"You'll need all the money you can get living abroad," Father Collin said, but I think it was just to stop me arguing with my mother.

I shook Father Collin's hand and when Miss Goff came out to say goodbye, I gave her a quick hug. "Thank you," I told her, and she blushed at my public embrace.

"You just remember us when you're playing in the London Orchestra or New York or somewhere," she said with a smile.

I laughed at the absurdity. "Deal."

They walked us out, I threw my bags in the boot of the car, and with one final look back, I waved goodbye.

WHEN WE GOT to Mum and Dad's, Mum asked me if I needed to pack anything else. But I figured if the two packed suitcases and everything in them had done me for the last year, it'd do me for the next.

As long as I had some clothes, my laptop, and my music books, I was good. I showed her the brochures and information on London's Royal Academy, and we googled London, looking at the city's landmarks, just out of curiosity.

I couldn't contain my excitement, and it showed. Mum smiled at me, but my stomach growled.

"What's for dinner?" I asked.

"I thought we could go out tonight."

"Oh." I couldn't hide my surprise. "Just us two? Why don't we get takeaway?" I suggested. "It'll be easier."

"No," she said. "Your father's told them he's taking the night off. He's picking up Holly from school. They'll be home soon," she said, looking at the clock. "We thought we would have a family dinner before you fly out in the morning."

"Mum," I said softly. "I don't feel like fighting with him tonight."

Mum patted my arm. "Don't be like that," she chided me. "He's making an effort."

Yeah well. We'd see about that.

Fifteen minutes later Dad and Holly arrived. Thirty minutes after that, when we were all dressed ready to go out, Dad put his phone on the hall stand. "Only Doctor Than knows where we're going. I told him to phone the restaurant only if it's an emergency he can't contain."

Huh.

That was a first.

And during dinner, I could tell he was trying to make an effort. He asked me about my exams and all about the school in London. He told me he paid the tuition at St. Michael's. Apparently me offering to use my own money to pay for high school made him realise just how serious I was.

I told them about Levi's family, who I'd basically be living with. I told them I'd be sharing the loft above the garage. "It's huge apparently, kinda like an apartment," I explained. "His Mum wanted to give him space, but also wants to keep an eye on him."

"She sounds like a smart woman," Mum said with a smile. "Levi seemed like a nice young man."

"He is, Mum," I agreed. When I felt myself blush a little, I tried to cover it by having a sip of my drink. Thankfully I was saved by the maître d', who came up to our table and addressed my parents by name. I quickly deduced they must come here often.

"You brought your children with you tonight?" he said with surprise.

I smiled, feeling like Exhibit A, and Holly gave him her best Goth sneer.

"Oh yes," Mum said with a plastered-on, well-practiced smile.

Dad then added, "Harrison sat his final exam today."

"He's off to London in the morning," Mum said.

The maître d' looked to me and said, "Oh, a vacation before University?"

"No," I explained. "I'm going to England for my music. I start next week."

"Ooooh," he said enthusiastically. "What is your instrument of choice?"

"Classical piano," Dad answered for me. I couldn't tell if he was proud, or if he was *pretending* to be proud.

"Oh, I love classical," the maître d' smiled with excited eyes. "You know, we have a piano here," he trailed off suggestively, pointing to the baby grand Steinway.

"Oh!" I said, stunned at the offer. I looked around at all the other restaurant guests. "I'm not sure I should do that."

"Yes, you can," he insisted. "If your parents don't mind, that is?" he asked, looking pointedly at my mother and father.

I shot a glance at my put-on-the-spot-parents. Mum dabbed the linen napkin to her mouth, obviously waiting for my dad to answer. Then Dad swallowed hard and said, "I'd like to hear you play."

And there it was. Finally. I'd played the piano since I was five years old and he had never, ever taken the time to hear me play. I smiled.

The maître d' led me toward the piano, and I took a seat and a deep breath. I'd played in front of crowds before, but I was incredibly nervous playing for my father. And when I looked up, I saw the other guests were quiet, watching me, waiting for me to play.

And so I played. Chopin's *Fantaisie-Impromptu*, because that's what this was.

I embraced the familiarity and comfort of playing the piano, and my shoulders relaxed as my fingers skimmed the keys. My emotions caught in every note. I breathed in the music. The door closing on one part of my life, the opening of another. A song of love and hope and new beginnings.

I got lost in how the sound filled my chest and my head. How it felt every time I played. And it wasn't until the last note floated heavy in the air that I even remembered the audience.

I looked around and saw my father first. His mouth was literally open, as if he couldn't believe what he'd just heard. But when the other guests started applauding—some were even standing—he looked at them, then back at me.

I stood up, gave a small bow and a nervous smile, and walked back to the table. Knowing most people were still watching me, I cleared my throat and took a drink of my Coke.

I looked at my mum, who was smiling hugely. Even Holly looked impressed. Then I looked at my dad. "Harrison," he said. His voice croaked, so he started again, "Harrison, I um... I had no idea." He shifted in his seat, and after a long moment, he said, "Your teacher was right; you deserve to be heard."

And after so many years of disagreeing and so many years of disappointment, his words filled my chest with pride.

"Thank you."

I BOARDED the plane and settled into my seat. Not even the thought of sixteen hours on a plane could dampen my spirits. Not even the woman beside me and her four-year-old brat could change my mood.

I was so fucking excited.

As soon as we were in the air, I put my earphones in to

drown out the sound of the screaming kid, pulled out my music pad, and went to my happy place.

Levi.

I figured sixteen hours stuck on a plane would give me plenty of time to write the music of my memories, of my hopes and dreams. The music of Levi.

So I started at the beginning.

I thought of him, his smile, his eyes, his laugh, and I wrote the music he made me feel. Levi's kiss, his hands, his scent, his taste. Page after page of him.

The lady beside me looked over and smiled. Whether she was referring to my smile or my notepad, I wasn't sure. "Must be someone special."

"Yeah."

"What's her name?" she asked, a seemingly innocent question.

"Levi," I answered.

"Oh," she said with a giggle. "Then *he* must be special."

I nodded and grinned at her. "He is."

And after I boarded the plane at eight in the morning, and sixteen torturously long hours later, the captain announced our descent into Heathrow. And if the trip on the plane took sixteen hours, then customs took a lifetime. But eventually, *e-fucking-ventually*, I walked through the terminal gates.

Lost and trying not to panic, I scanned the crowd looking for him, and as I turned around, I was hit by a tall, sandy-blond, smelling-fucking-divine Levi. His arms were around me, holding me so tight. "Oh, my God," he mumbled into my neck. "You're really here. You're really, really here!"

God, it felt good to feel him against me. Everything that was familiar, that was perfect and better than I'd remembered, was in my arms. I held him just as tight and laughed, "Yeah, I'm really here."

Levi pulled away and cupped my face in his hands. I forgot I didn't have to hide who I was anymore. I forgot everything, except for him. And I held his face and kissed him.

He was all fair skin, flushed cheeks, and smiling eyes. He was everything, and he was in my arms, and any "what the hell am I doing" doubts flitted away. I knew I'd done the right thing. This was *exactly* where I was supposed to be. I'd been in London for mere minutes, but I was home.

CHAPTER 8

LONDON

I DON'T KNOW how or when it happened, but the first year flew.

I had no delusions it was going to be easy. I knew I was in for hellish studies and would need a commitment to my music that I wouldn't have thought humanly possible. Doing my bachelor's degree at London's Royal Academy of Music was far and away the most daunting thing I'd ever done. I had grades to make to keep my scholarship and expectations to exceed.

I also knew that living with Levi wasn't going to be easy either. When he'd said he lived above the garage, I pictured a large loft-style open area. Apparently garages in Australia were bigger than those in England, because if I stood with my arms outstretched, I could almost touch the side walls. It was a long narrow room with a double bed up one end, a lounge and TV in the middle, and a bathroom at the other end. It was smaller than a one-bedroom studio, but it was ours and it was perfect.

His university course was demanding as well, and we knew our different schools would lead us in different directions, timetables, social circles. Everything was different. The time we had together when not studying for exams was limited, and most of the time we were both exhausted.

But somehow we made it work.

I loved my music more now than I ever had.

I also loved Levi in ways that surprised me.

No, life with him wasn't easy. It wasn't perfect. Life wasn't some soap opera episode of Gays of Our Lives. It was real, and sometimes brutally unforgiving. Some days there were arguments. Some days we didn't see each other at all. But some days we laughed and talked until after midnight and did the tourist, sight-seeing thing for me. Some days we made love for hours and lounged in front of a movie, wrapped around each other.

Life in England was more different to Australia than I realised it would be. The weather mostly, and Levi would often joke that me wearing so many layers was akin to a game of pass the parcel—just more wrapping to take off, he'd say. But it was living with his family that I found the strangest. I'd lived at a boarding school for the last six years, and before that we had a nanny, so to have an actual mum and dad around took some getting used to. Sitting around a table and eating as a family was something I thought only happened in movies, but apparently it was common practice in the Aston household.

Levi's family took me in like I was one of them, from the very first day. His brother Jared was funny, and his sister Lila clearly thought we were cute together because she told us at least once a week. His dad would cuss at the football on TV, and his mum would hug and feed me whenever she saw me. I had to admit, I loved it.

And maybe living in a different country made things different between me and my parents, because we actually had phone calls to each other. Calls were always brief, and not all that often, but it was a start.

Which was why Levi and I were back at Heathrow and I was nervous. Levi gave my hand a squeeze. "It'll be fine," he said, for the fiftieth time.

The screen of arrivals showed their plane had landed, and we were waiting for my mother and sister to come through the gates. My father would join us next week, just in time to watch my final performance of the year, which also happened to be my final practical exam. Something I was trying not to think about.

"Oh, look at you, love," Mrs Aston said, with a look of worry on her face. "What are you in such a panic for? They'll be so excited to see you!"

Levi squeezed my hand again and waited for me to answer, but when I couldn't, he did. "Harrison's family don't know about us," he said, holding up our joined hands.

"They don't even know I'm gay," I mumbled.

Mrs Aston knew this. I guessed she just forgot. Her face fell. "Oh, love."

"Harrison thinks I'll hate him for having to act like we're just friends," Levi added with a smile. "I've told him not to be daft. It's just a week."

I sighed. "I still feel bad." I looked him in the eye. "I'll tell them. Before they leave, I'll tell them. I promise."

"Hey," he said, suddenly serious. His eyebrows knitted together and his blue eyes pierced into mine. "You're not doing anything you're not comfortable doing, especially on account of me, you hear? I've told you this a hundred times."

"Levi," I started, but he shook his head.

"Not this week. You've got too much stress as it is.

Exams, studies, family visiting. I think that's enough to deal with, 'kay?"

I sighed, and the first flood of people came through the gates. There were people getting hugged and kissed, there was laughter and tears. Then I saw them: my mother and sister were toward the back, anxiously scanning the crowd. I gave Levi's hand one last squeeze. "I'm sorry," I told him and let go of his hand.

CHAPTER 9

MY MOTHER WAS the most emotional I think I'd ever seen her. She hugged me, then put her hand to my face and looked up at me with tears in her eyes. "Oh, look at you! You look so good!"

I blushed at her compliment, quickly kissing her cheek before I pulled Holly in for a hug. She was still dressed in black, though the bright purple laces in her high Doc Martins matched the streak of purple in her hair perfectly. I was even afforded a smile.

"You guys remember Levi?" I asked, motioning toward him. "And this is his mum, Mrs Aston."

Mrs Aston surprised my mother by hugging her. "Please, call me Valerie."

"Thank you so much for having Harrison in your home," my mother said, squeezing Mrs Aston's hand. "For taking care of him."

"Oh, it's no bother. He's been an absolute pleasure to have."

Levi coughed and smiled, and I knew he was agreeing

with his mother—though their interpretations of pleasure were vastly different.

"How was your trip?" I asked them, trying to divert their attention. "Not too long and boring?"

"No, no," Mum said. "It was fine. Though we didn't sleep at all."

"Then we better get you checked into your hotel," I said. "Let me grab your luggage."

"Yes, I must apologise again for not having the room at our house," Mrs Aston said. "My kids just won't leave."

Levi put his arm around his mum as we walked out of the airport. "That's because you look after us too good, Ma."

It said a lot about our family dynamics, as the two Aston's walked out with their arms around each other, and the three Haddon's walked with a good metre between each of us. I don't think my mother even noticed, but Levi's mum certainly did.

After we'd checked them into their hotel, we said we'd wait downstairs in the lobby to give them some time to get unpacked and freshen up. As soon as my mother and sister disappeared through the elevator doors, Mrs Aston hugged me fiercely. "You okay, love?"

"Yeah, I'm fine," I told her.

She held my arms and tilted her head. "Not real close to them, are you?"

I shook my head. "No."

"You know, raising kids isn't that hard," she said with a shake of her head. "Just have to feed them every now and then and let them know they're loved."

Her words hit me harder than they should have, and my eyes burned with tears because she made it sound so simple, when in my family, it was anything but. "Okay Mum," Levi said, pulling me out of her hands and into his arms. His embrace was a healing thing. His warmth was a balm to the ache in my chest. He kissed the side of my neck. "You okay, babe?"

I nodded. "Yeah. I am now."

He rubbed my back. "They're here, that's the important part. They're making an effort. So let's show them a good time, hey?"

I nodded and pulled back so I could peck his lips. "Thank you."

"And don't be worrying about telling them about us," Levi added. "They're only here for a week, and I've got you all year."

"You do," I told him.

He grinned. "Two four seven, three six five, baby."

That made me smile, as always. "I've gotten so used to not hiding anything," I admitted. "I can be me here." It was true. I started college as an out-and-proud gay man, I walked downtown holding Levi's hand, we went to pubs with friends as a couple. I had no one to hide from in London. Every single person who I couldn't be myself in front of—who, ironically, were my family—lived on the other side of the planet. Except now they were upstairs and staying for a week. And after a whole year, you'd think I'd have missed them, and in some ways I did, but there was also an unease in my chest at them being here. I didn't mean to seem ungrateful, I was glad to see them. I just kept waiting for the axe to fall.

I didn't even want to think about when my father got here. Though I wondered whether he would even show. Maybe there'd be some emergency and he'd miss his flight.

Levi put his hand to my face. "It's just a week. They'll be sightseeing, we'll be studying. They're staying here, we'll be at home."

I nodded, just as Mrs Aston said, "If you've got a problem with it, I suggest you keep your bloody mouth as closed as your mind."

Levi and I both turned to find some old woman scurrying away, clutching her pearls, looking all sorts of offended, and Mrs Aston was smiling after her. Levi and I broke apart laughing and he gave his mum a hug. "Oh, Mum."

"You know I can't stand people who think they're better than everyone else," she said with an unapologetic shrug.

Good Lord. And she was about to spend the day with my mother...

Just then, Mum and Holly came into the lobby. Our laughter died away and Mum smiled at us. "So, where to first?"

"I was thinking I could show you around my campus?" I suggested. "Then we can grab something to eat then you guys can sleep off some jetlag."

My mother smiled. "Sounds great."

I ACTUALLY THINK my mother was impressed with my school, and impressing her was no small feat. "The main hall is through there. That's where you'll be watching the finals," I explained. "The studio I use is up through here."

I led the way with my mother and sister, and Levi and his mum followed close behind.

"Hey, Harrison," Kim called out. "Good luck on Friday."

"Thanks. Same to you. Oh, have you seen Prishna? She wanted to swap studio times with me, that's all."

"Not today," Kim replied. "Need her number?"

"No, I have it. Thanks."

She kept on her way, then we were met by other students who all smiled and called me by name, which was weird—only for the fact I'm sure my mother felt out of place that these complete strangers probably knew me better than she did. Or that I had a life here, school and friends that she had no clue about.

"You know a lot of people," she commented.

"I spend a lot of time here," I replied.

"I love the buildings," Holly said. "They're so old! We don't have *old* buildings in Sydney. Our whole country is only two-hundred years old."

"Ah," Levi pounced. "Let me show you something really special. It's in the park," he said, leading Holly off to show her the villas, no doubt.

Mrs Aston laughed. "That boy and architecture. I hope she won't mind getting her ear chewed off."

I laughed at that. If there was one thing Levi could talk about, that was how buildings were built. "I'm sure he's already explaining mason construction techniques of the seventeenth century."

Mrs Aston laughed and Mum smiled, but it didn't quite sit well on her face. We spent the next little while just walking through Regent's Park taking in the grounds and gardens, until we met up with Levi and Holly. They were both smiling, like they could become fast friends, and that warmed my heart.

We found a little café, and I deliberately positioned us so I sat with Holly. The mothers sat on one side, and Levi sat at the corner spot, buffering their mother-type conversation while I got some private time with my sister.

"So, tell me, what's news in Sydney?"

She couldn't tell me much. It wasn't like we had friends

in common. We hadn't even lived under the same roof for seven years. But I kept pushing. "How's school?"

"Ugh," she groaned. "I go back just in time to start trials."

I groaned in sympathy. Trial HSC exams were the precursor to the real thing, and just as bad. "What are you hoping to do when you leave?" I asked, taking a sip of my drink.

"Um, pre-med."

I almost choked on my drink. "Really? You do?"

She almost smiled. "Yeah."

"Bet Dad's happy with that?"

Holly shrugged. "Not sure he even knows."

"What?"

She glanced at our mother, who was still caught up in conversation with Mrs Aston. "Don't think he cares, to be honest. I'm the *daughter*, remember?" She said it like it was a dirty word. "His expectations for me are to probably join the Women's Auxiliary and do fundraising and work the social calendar like Mum."

I leaned in and whispered, "Fuck him."

Holly blinked in surprise.

"I'm serious, Holly. You be whatever it is you wanna be. A hairdresser, a backpacker, a politician, a doctor, whatever. Don't let him tell you what to do with your life." I sat back and smiled at her. "And for what it's worth, I think you'd make a great doctor."

"I need to get an ATAR of ninety-six," she said.

"How do you think you'll go?" Levi asked.

"Well, my year advisor thinks I'll get higher," she answered, as though it was no big deal.

"Jesus, Holly," I said with a snort. "Genius, much?"

"Harrison," my mother chided. "Language, please."

I rolled my eyes and Holly grinned into her drink, and I knew right then that even though my sister and I were never particularly close, that we'd be okay.

"So," Mrs Aston intervened. "Harrison, I was just telling your mother how much you've been studying. You both have," she nodded pointedly at Levi.

"Five days to go," I said. "I have my final theory exam in two days, then the practical, which you will all bear witness to. God help me if I fu... fail."

Levi scoffed out a laugh at my almost-Freudian slip. "You can't fail. You're brilliant and your professor knows it."

"Yes," I conceded, "but everyone in my class is brilliant. I need to be *more* brilliant."

"Jeez, Harrison," Holly said. "Perfectionist, much?"

I feigned offence while Levi burst out laughing. "Oh my God, you have no idea."

DINNER WAS AWKWARD. Levi's parents were their usual courteous, polite selves, and I rather enjoyed spending time with Holly. But my mother wore her fake on-show, I'm-better-than-you smile. She was nice enough, but I had the distinct impression she had to try very hard to be there.

Maybe it was just me. Maybe it was my insecurities that made me feel that way. Everyone else seemed to be having a great time, but I spent the entire night on edge, waiting for my mother to sniff delicately and declare she was tired. She didn't though.

Yet I still felt hugely inadequate. I wanted them to get along. I wanted her to see Levi and his family for the good people they are. Not that I could explain to my mother why

I wanted her to like them, but it was important to me none-theless.

I sat next to Holly, across from Levi, and the three of us talked while the parents at the table chatted away.

"You okay?" Levi asked quietly. Only me and Holly heard him.

"Sure," I replied. "Just tired."

Levi's eyes flinched a little, which was his silent way of calling bullshit. Instead of pressing me further, he turned to my sister. "So, pre-med, yeah? What do you think you'll specialise in?"

"I'm still not certain, but I'm leaning toward cardiology," she said. She inhaled deeply and let it out with a sigh. "It's ironic isn't it? That it's what he wanted you to do and it became this whole big issue. Yet, it's what I want to be, and he hasn't even asked."

"Do whatever makes you happy," I told her again.

Levi smiled knowingly. "It took me a while to convince Harrison to do the same," he explained.

"And for him to apply to a music school in a different country on my behalf without my knowledge or consent," I added.

He grinned at me. "It worked, didn't it?"

I found myself smiling at him. "It sure did."

Holly looked from me to Levi and back again, and I could see the penny drop in her eyes. *She knew.* Cold fingers of dread tickled down my spine and knotted in my stomach. She knew there was something going on between us. She blushed a little but sipped her drink, and before I could scramble together something to say, my mother inter-rupted. "Thank you for a lovely evening, but it's getting late."

"Yeah, we have exams to study for," I added, needing to change topics.

My mother air-kissed everyone's cheek, I got a big hug from Holly, and we all went home.

When we made it into the Aston family kitchen, I turned to Levi's parents. "Thank you for tonight. I hope my mother wasn't too snooty."

Mrs Aston laughed. "She was very lovely," she said.

"But?"

"No buts," she said. "I think she really wants to be a part of your life, but isn't quite sure how to go about it." Mrs Aston frowned. "It's quite sad really. I couldn't imagine being so detached from my kids."

Levi hugged her. "Neither could I."

Mrs Aston smiled warmly. "Can I make you boys a pot of tea?"

"No thanks, Mum," Levi said, taking my hand. "We're off to bed."

"I thought you said you had to study," Mr Aston said, looking directly at me.

Levi laughed. "We do. But I never mentioned books." He pulled me down the hall.

I heard Mrs Aston chastise him, "Oh, Levi," as we went up the stairs, though there was a smile in her voice.

When the door was closed behind us, Levi turned and his smile slowly faded. "You okay?"

I nodded. "I am now."

"It wasn't too bad, and Holly's great."

"I think she knows," I said. "She was looking at us funny."

Levi nodded. "I saw that. But she was fine. And you know what?" he asked. "Maybe that's enough for now. Maybe you don't have to tell your parents anything just yet.

You're just getting things back on track with them, so one thing at a time maybe?"

I shrugged. "I want them to know me. The real me."

He kissed me softly. "Whenever you're ready."

I put my hands to his face. "Take me to bed, Levi."

He hummed and it sounded almost like a purr. "Oh yes, I have a study date with your body."

I kissed him again, slower this time, and pulled his bottom lip between mine. "Where will you start?"

He smiled like the devil, and walked me backwards until I fell onto my back on the bed. He pulled off my shoes. "I'll start at the beginning."

By the time he had me undressed and ready for him, I was writhing with want and need. I was stretched and aching with desire. "I need you," I whispered.

"Need you too," he replied with a trail of kisses down my neck. "You're so perfect."

I ran my fingers through his hair and down his back. "Need you inside me."

He pulled back and smiled, his lips swollen and wet. "You have such magical fingers."

I spread my legs and rolled my hips, rubbing our erections together. "Levi, please."

He leaned back on his knees and added more lube to his hand. He gave himself more strokes, and then with his hands on my hips, he pulled me onto his thighs. He aligned the head of his cock against my waiting arsehole and slowly pushed into me.

We'd stopped using condoms after our tests at the sex clinic came back, giving us the all clear. It was a natural step for us; there was something extremely intimate about not using condoms with him. Intimate and fucking hot. I couldn't deny it—feeling him swell and come deep inside me turned me on.

I'd never felt closer to him.

I sucked back a breath as he breached me, stretched me, and pushed further into me. But he read my body's cues, he held me tight and he waited.

When I couldn't wait any longer, when my body needed him to move, I all but begged him. "Please."

Levi settled his weight above me and hooked his arms around the backs of my thighs. He lifted my legs higher toward our chests and started to thrust slowly in and out of me. He ghosted his lips over mine, never taking his eyes off me. This was us; well-practised, well-rehearsed. We fit together like a jigsaw puzzle, interlocking, making the whole picture complete.

He pushed in deeper, until he was fully seated inside me, and he stopped. His nostrils flared with the exertion it took not to move, but he stared into my eyes and kissed me softly.

"I belong here," I whispered.

He answered with a soft kiss. "With me."

"Always."

His breath hitched and he throbbed inside me. "Don't hold back," I said gruffly. "Make me yours."

He closed his eyes and flexed his hips, pushing up into me as deep as he could. When his eyes opened, his pupils were blown and there was a fire inside him. I could see it: burning love and desire.

His mouth opened, his cheeks flushed pink down his neck, and with a strangled cry, he came.

I reached between us and took my own cock in my hand, and just a few quick strokes sent my orgasm rolling through me.

Levi kissed me deeply, tenderly, until my head stopped spinning. He rolled us over and wrapped me in his arms. "Love you," I murmured.

Just before I fell asleep, Levi pressed his lips to my head. "Two four seven, three six five."

CHAPTER 10

THE NEXT DAY was spent with our heads in books. Mum and Holly were spending the time shopping so, thankfully, there was no pressure on me to entertain them. I really needed to get my revision notes memorised. Levi and I helped each other, only taking breaks in our own study to help the other with pop quizzes and essay briefs.

We worked well together. We always had. Even though we were in completely different fields, I knew how his mind ticked, and he did mine. We only stopped when Mrs Aston brought up sandwiches, and then dived straight back into it.

I went into my final theory exam confident and was so relieved when it was all over. Levi was happy with how his exams had gone as well, and it felt like a weight had been lifted—I only had one exam to go, and I'd almost forgotten about my father arriving the next day.

But we—being me, Levi, Holly, and my mother—went to Heathrow to welcome him. I had a mix of emotions as we waited for him to come through the gates. I was excited: I wanted him to see how happy I was here, and I wanted him to see that choosing music was the best thing for me. I was also excited just to see him. It had been a year, after all.

I was also nervous: I knew there was a chance he still thought the whole 'playing piano for a living' was a whimsical dream—maybe that's why he was coming. So he could watch me fail with his own two eyes. Or maybe I was being unfair... Maybe he was genuinely happy for me. He had taken almost ten days off work to visit, and that was a first. Ever. So I *was* grateful, but I was also waiting for that snide comment to knock me down a peg or two.

After eighteen years of hearing it, I'd come to expect it.

Admittedly, when he did come through the gates, it was good to see him. He looked like he might have actually slept on the plane, and in hindsight, it was probably the longest he'd gone without being called or paged since the invention of such devices.

My mother hugged him, which was the most emotionally animated I'd ever seen them. I know most teenagers had trouble seeing their parents show affection, but these were *my* parents, who rarely showed any affection at all. To anyone.

It was weird.

It was also a little reminder that their kids didn't rate as high as their spouse on their ladder of "reasons to show affection."

I wasn't the only one who thought as much. I could see a familiar sting in Holly's eyes when my father gave Holly a one-armed, side-on awkward hug. All I was gifted with was a firm handshake, Levi got no more than a nod, but my thoughts were with Holly. In all this, I had Levi. In my final year of school, I had someone to share the hurt of rejection with, but she didn't. I put my arm around her as we walked out. "Wanna come back to our place?" I asked her quietly.

"We'll do something fun this afternoon before we all go out for dinner tonight."

She looked up at me with a spark of hope in her eyes. "You have to study, don't you?"

Levi answered. "He knows Beethoven better than he knows himself. He'll be fine."

Holly grinned. "That'd be great."

———

I KNEW IT WAS RISKY. I knew by showing Holly our room, I was outing myself to her. There was, after all, just one bed.

But she never mentioned it. "Cool," she said, walking into our loft above the garage. "It's just like a dorm room."

"Yeah, but my mum cooks for us," Levi told her. He flopped down onto the unmade bed. "And does our washing."

Holly stared at him. "Your mum does washing?"

I snorted. Yes, it was clear the Aston's had money, but Mrs Aston wouldn't dream of letting anyone else cook or clean for her family. "Yeah, imagine having a mother that does stuff for you. Levi's mum spends her life fussing over her kids."

Holly laughed incredulously. Then she spied some movies next to the TV. "Oh, you have the real Avengers!"

I groaned. "It's not the Marvel version. It's the poxy British version."

Holly picked up the cover. "I can see that, dumb arse." Levi busted up laughing at my facial expression. Holly smiled at him. "Can we watch it?"

"'Course!" he said. "I love Cathy Gale!"

"Oh, I know, right?" Holly said. "Everyone only remembers Emma Peel, but Cathy was so much better."

I sighed the longest suffering sigh I could manage, which earned me a glare from both of them. "I'll go make some popcorn," I told them. "Feel free to start without me."

I went downstairs and rifled through the pantry for some popcorn when Mrs Aston found me. "I'll fix it for you," she said and was already pulling bowls out before I could argue.

"I don't mind," I offered. "They're watching The Avengers."

Mrs Aston laughed. "Holly's a sweet thing."

"She is."

"You're a lot alike," she added. "And you have a lot in common."

"True. We understand the whole dysfunctional family thing."

She looked at me for a long moment. "Can I give you my opinion?" she asked.

"Of course."

"Your parents love you," she said simply. "They're just closed off. Maybe their parents were exactly the same. But it will stop with you and Holly. When you and Levi have kids, you'll be the best dads ever."

I almost swallowed my tongue. "Kids?" I squeaked. "What?"

She laughed. "You're too young now," she said as she poured the kernels into the pan. "But one day. Parenting skills are usually passed on from one generation to the next. Good and bad traits, mind you. You know what it's like to have to earn your parents approval, and there's no way you'd do that to your own child."

My mind was still stuck on the word *kids*.

Mrs Aston took one look at me and laughed. "Go on, love. Upstairs with you. I'll bring this up when it's done. Oh, and Harrison, just so you know, I'd be pleased as punch if and when you and Levi decide you want to start a family."

I think I squeaked again as some kind of response and bolted up to our room.

"Hey," Levi said, looking from the TV to me. "Where's the popcorn?" Then he looked at my face again. "What's wrong?"

I plonked myself down onto the sofa so Holly was in between us. "Nothing. Your mum is fixing us snacks. Real popcorn, not the microwave stuff."

Ten minutes later, Mrs Aston brought up a tray with a bowl of popcorn and a jug of juice. She handed the bowl to Holly. "Here you go, love."

"Oh, thank you so much," Holly said quickly.

"No problem," Mrs Aston said. Then she looked at Levi, who had taken a handful of popcorn and shoved it in his mouth. "Did Harrison tell you how we talked about him having kids?"

Levi choked.

I looked around Holly to Levi. "She talked. I died inside."

Mrs Aston just laughed then noticed the TV. "Oh, I always liked Cathy," as she walked out, closing the door behind her.

Holly burst out laughing. "Levi, I think I love your mum. This is the best popcorn I've ever had."

DINNER with my father there was different than when it

was just Mum and Holly. Levi's parents weren't there, so the attention wasn't buffered like it was before. Mum seemed to notch up the performance of perfect wife/perfect family, and Dad seemed surprised by Levi being there, though asking him twenty questions was clearly a lot easier than asking me.

Maybe Mrs Aston was right. Maybe my father didn't speak to me very often because he didn't know how. He could ask a virtual stranger two dozen questions, but his son? It didn't appear so.

Did he think I would bite his head off? Did he have more to lose by getting it wrong with me? I just didn't know.

"Isn't that right, Harrison?" Levi asked. It was his sixth attempt at trying to include me in conversation. When it was obvious I had no clue what he was talking about, he repeated, "That your final theory exam went well. His professor thinks he's the brightest student he's seen in a long time."

"Oh," I mumbled, fidgeting in my seat. "Yeah. Um, yeah. It's a relief to be done. Just one more to go. The big recital." My lip pulled down in one corner. "I'm nervous that you guys will be there."

"I'm sure you'll be fine," my mother said.

Dad sipped his wine. "So, your theory exam? What was that about?"

"My last exam was a history overview, which covers music and composers from medieval times to present."

My father blinked, then schooled his features. "How do you feel it went?" he asked.

"Fine," I answered, trying to ignore the feeling of scrutiny. "It was on Renaissance, Baroque, Rococo, and Classical, and how those periods influenced music in the twenty-first century."

It was a topic I could talk about at length, forever. Though I knew it would bore most people, so I toned it down. But it was easy conversation for me. All my parents had to do was nod and smile, and I got to talk about what I loved. It wasn't as complex as cardiothoracic surgery, but I'd hoped my passion showed through.

My father even smiled.

It was like a reward to me—as stupid as that sounded and as stupid as that felt—but even the slightest hint of approval meant a lot to me. And by the time dinner was done, I felt more comfortable in the company of my parents than I had in a long time. Or possibly ever.

"I'm afraid jetlag has caught up with me," Dad said, biting back a yawn. "What's your plans for tomorrow?"

"I have a studio booked for a two-hour practice session before the final," I answered.

"And the exam is scheduled for eleven the day after?" he asked.

The fact he'd remembered made me smile. "Yes."

"I'm looking forward to it," he said. "But I have to get some sleep." He looked at our fresh cups of tea. "Stay. Finish your drinks. I'll fix the bill up on my way out," he said, standing up. He buttoned his jacket and waited for my mother to straighten her chair.

"I'll be in touch tomorrow," Mum said, and with a wave from Holly, they left.

I think I sat there for a full twenty seconds and never said anything. I was trying to process what had just happened.

"So?" Levi asked eventually.

I turned to him and laughed. "Oh my God. I think we just had a normal family dinner. He didn't say a great deal to me, but still, it was civil."

"No fighting," Levi added.

"Not once," I said. "That's like some kind of record."

Levi put his hand on my thigh and smiled brilliantly. "Babe, I'm so happy for you."

I couldn't help it, and I did it without thinking. I leaned in and pressed my lips to his. It wasn't anything lewd, just a press of smiling lips, but I had that awful feeling that someone was watching. With a sense of dread, I turned to see my father. He must have come back in to tell me something, or maybe he forgot something.... He was standing there, stunned. Horrified. Disgusted. He opened his mouth and promptly snapped it shut. He raised his hand then let it drop to his side. He shook his head and turned to walk away.

I wasn't going to follow him.

I wasn't going to run, chase him down and tell him what? I was sorry? And apologise for who I was?

"Shit," Levi mumbled. He took off to follow my father. "Doctor Haddon!"

I grabbed Levi's arm. Well, as much as I didn't want to run after him, it'd be a cold day in hell before I let Levi do it. "I'll go."

I went after my father and saw him disappear through the front doors as I entered the lobby. I got to the doors and called, "Dad?"

He faltered but didn't stop.

"Dad, wait!"

The London street was wet and dark. There were cars parked at the kerb, and the people walking on the footpaths were huddled with umbrellas in the misting rain. But my father just kept walking.

And it pissed me off that he thought he could just walk away. "Stop!"

He spun on his heel. His eyes were wild. "What do you want me to say, Harrison?"

His anger surprised me, though it seemed to feed my own. "How about 'well shit, didn't see that coming' or 'we knew before you did' or even 'you're such a fucking disappointment.' Anything. Say anything, but do not walk away."

He took a step closer and pointed his finger at me. "You should have said something."

"Ha!" I scoffed, ignoring the rain. "And willingly start this pleasant conversation?"

"We deserved to be told," he cried. "After everything we've done for you!"

"Deserved? Well, that's fucking rich. Deserved what? Two children you don't even know?" I yelled. "Do you think pouring money into an expensive school makes you a good father? What about five minutes? You know in six years of high school, I can count on one hand the times I spent more than ten minutes with you. So you know what? You get exactly what you deserve."

I was so angry. I was angry for every time he brushed me off, for every time he made me feel like I was never good enough. Maybe having this conversation in the street, in the rain, wasn't ideal, but it was happening, and I couldn't stop myself. Nineteen years of constant disappointment finally bubbled over.

"So I'm gay. I don't care what you think about that, because I refuse to apologise. I'm not sorry for who I am. And I'm not sorry for loving Levi. Because he is the best thing to ever happen to me."

I held up two fingers. "There are only two people in this world who have ever believed in me." I pointed back to the restaurant. "Levi is one. And my old teacher, Miss Goff. A fucking school teacher! They're the only two people who never doubted me. Not my parents. Oh, hell no." I shook my head. "Have you ever even asked Holly what she wants to do with her life?"

He stared at me blankly.

"I won't ruin the surprise for you, but at least you'll have one child that's not a bitter disappointment."

"You were never a disappointment," he said quietly. The fight in him was gone. "Do you really hate me that much? Did I get it so wrong?"

I pulled at my hair. "I don't hate you." My breath left me in a rush. "I don't hate you. I hate that I will never be good enough."

He shook his head, a deep frown etched on his face. The rain made him look as old as I'd ever seen him. "I have never said you weren't."

"You said that every time you told me my dreams were stupid. You said it every time you missed a birthday party, every time work was more important."

He opened his mouth but decided against whatever it was he was going to say. Still frowning, he took a step back and nodded. Then he turned and walked away. Like he'd just disqualified my hurt and anger, like he always did, like it didn't mean a thing.

I watched him until he disappeared, and every fucking cell in my body burned with a rage. An anger I could no longer contain festered and erupted, and with a scream of frustration and vitriol, I closed my fist and swung at the streetlight. I knew as soon as I'd punched the steel pole, with the searing pain that shot through my hand and up my arm, that I'd done some damage.

Then Levi was there holding me up, and I was crying, and I was still so fucking mad. I just wanted to go home. I wanted to crawl into bed with him where it was warm and perfect, where he could hold me and tell me everything would be okay.

But he didn't.

He took me to the hospital. Two days before the most important piano performance of my life, and I'd just broken my hand.

CHAPTER 11

I SAT on the hospital bed as the doctor examined my right hand. Levi was sitting out in the waiting room, and I'd never wanted him by my side more than I had in that very moment. I had two cuts across my knuckles, but they weren't my greatest concern. The x-rays on the light board to my right showed two fractured bones.

"What did you punch?" the doctor asked.

"A streetlight."

"Well, that'd do it. There's not much give in streetlights."

"No, there's not," I mumbled.

"Wanna tell me why you went all Rocky Balboa on a defenceless steel pole?"

I swallowed hard. "I had a... disagreement with my father."

The doctor nodded like he'd heard it all before. "Well, what you have here is called a boxer's fracture," the doctor said. He expertly felt along my hand at the bones that aligned my ring and pinky fingers. "Though I don't know why it's called that, because boxers usually know how to punch without breaking their hands," he mused casually. "They also don't punch streetlights."

I would have sighed if he wasn't hurting my hand so much.

"There's angulation of the metacarpal bones," he said. "Which means—"

"I know what it means," I said quietly. "My father's a doctor."

The doctor was quiet for a moment. He stilled his fingers on my hand.

"They're not too bad, but they'll need to be realigned."

I nodded. "Can you just do it now?"

"I can administer some more pain relief—" he started to say, but I shook my head.

"I'm fine," I lied. My voice was so quiet and detached, I barely recognised it. "But my... friend that brought me here, can he come in? Please? His name is Levi Aston. I'd just rather go home, so if we can just get it over with, that'd be great. But I'd really appreciate it if he could be here when you realign my hand."

The doctor was quiet, and whether it was the way my voice cracked or the tears that fell down my cheeks, I don't know, but he let go of my hand and disappeared through the door. He came back in a moment later with a tentative Levi following right behind him.

He stuck his head around the door, looking all worried, but when he saw my face, he rushed straight in. He took my good hand in one of his and pulled me against him. He kissed the side of my head. "You okay?" I shook my head against his chest.

"I have to realign the bones," the doctor said, taking my right hand. I didn't know if he was shocked or disgusted at us, because I didn't look up.

"Oh Jesus," Levi murmured and he held me a little tighter.

The doctor deftly felt along the palm, and with a quick push and pull and shooting pain, it was done.

He made me move my fingers and asked me to close my fist. It hurt like a bitch. It stung and ached at the same time and even made me feel a bit queasy. "Okay, so we can do one of two things," the doctor explained. "A cast or a splint."

"Splint," I answered quickly. "I have my final exams the day after tomorrow, so I'll need to take the splint off to play."

"Play what?" the doctor asked.

"Piano. I'm a first-year at the Royal Academy of Music," I answered. "Playing the piano is what I do."

"Harrison," Levi said softly, looking at my now-purple and banged up hand. "You can't play…"

I looked up at him. "I have to. I don't have a choice. I sit the exam or I fail, broken hand or not."

Levi frowned. "You could apply for an extension, or surely a medical reason would be enough."

"Then what?" I asked. "There's a dozen people lined up behind me to take my place. I can't lose my scholarship, Levi, because then I can't stay at school. I have my Grand-mother's trust money, but I use that to live, not pay for school. I can't lose my place in school. I just can't." I blinked back more tears. "If I fail, then he wins. He gets to say he was right all along. He'll have me back in Sydney at fucking medical school." I looked at the doctor. "No offence."

He tried not to smile as he held up the splint. "None taken. You know there are better careers than being a lowly doctor. I hear streetlight punching is a great profession these days."

I snorted out a laugh, despite the tears in my eyes.

"Point taken. God, I was so stupid to hit that post. I've never punched anything in my life."

Levi held up my left hand and inspected my fingers. "I dunno. I've seen you bang away at the piano until your hands ached and your fingers almost bled."

The doctor held my wrist and fixed the splint. "Well, I have to say, these are not fighting hands. With fingers this long, I would have guessed you were destined to be a piano player or a surgeon."

"Cardiothoracic surgeon, to be more precise," I added. "And believe me, the irony of a doctor telling me my piano playing days are over is not lost on me."

The doctor finished bandaging the splint in place. "We're not all bad, you know."

"I know," I amended poorly. "I'm sorry. I don't mean anything by it. I'm just... feeling very sorry for myself, and very stupid right about now."

The doctor sighed. "I understand your position, but I have to say it goes against any medical advice given by me or this hospital that you play the piano in two days."

"Actually, I have a two hour studio session scheduled for tomorrow," I admitted. I glanced up at Levi. "I swapped with Prishna, remember?"

"Doc," Levi said. "Is there something he can take to kill the pain? He's gonna play the piano regardless of what you and I, or anyone else, says. So, is there something he can do to make it bearable?"

"Or numb," I said. "Because the ache is killing me."

The doctor's tone was stronger now, all joking was gone. "Keep it elevated. I'll fit a sling to keep it above your heart. You can take ibuprofen and paracetamol together, but only the recommended doses. If the swelling gets worse or it feels numb or cold, you need to come right back here, okay?

Bruising is expected, so is pain. You broke your hand, that's going to hurt. You can expect to keep this splint on for four to six weeks. Taking it off," he looked at his watch, "in a matter of hours and stressing that hand by doing something for extended periods of time—like playing the piano—could do more long term damage. Now I can administer a cortisone injection and it might reduce the swelling and help with pain, but it could also impede all movement for up to forty-eight hours. Or you could have a shot of Marcaine. It'll kill the pain, but your hand will also be numb. In which case, you won't be playing anything."

I looked up at Levi, searching his eyes for an answer. All I found was worry and concern. "No injections. I can't risk it. I'll be fine," I added quickly, as Levi started to object. "I just have to get through these two days, then I have the whole summer to heal."

Levi frowned, but he nodded. "I'm really sorry it turned out the way it did tonight," he said gently. "I'm sure he'll come around."

I swallowed down the lump in my throat. "I'm not sure if I want him to. I think I'm done. I'm just... done."

Levi ran his hand through my hair and pulled my face against his chest. He kissed the top of my head and sighed. "Can we please go home? My mum's probably got her knickers in a twist by now."

I pulled back. "You told her?"

"Of course I did. She's worried sick about you!"

The thought of Mrs Aston sitting in her kitchen with a tea cup in her hand waiting for us made me sigh. "I don't want her to worry."

Levi put his hand to my face. "Your family might be dysfunctional and emotionally despondent, but mine loves you, Harrison. Get used to it, okay?"

I finally managed a smile. "'kay."

IT WASN'T JUST Mrs Aston who was waiting up, but Levi's dad as well. As soon as we walked through the door, Mrs Aston was on her feet with worry and sadness etched into her eyes. "Oh, you poor boy," she said soothingly, with her hands to my face. "And your hand! Is it really broken? What did the doctor say? Come in and I'll make you some fresh tea."

"Mum," Levi interjected. "Harrison just really wants to go to bed. It's been a long day."

"No, it's okay," I said. I looked his parent's right in the eyes. "Thank you, for waiting up, for caring. It's more than I..." *ever got, ever deserved.* "I just really appreciate it."

"Oh, love," Mrs Aston said with glassy eyes. "Of course we'd wait up."

Levi took my good hand and led me to the hall, but before we could leave, Mr Aston's voice stopped me. "Harrison," he said, walking over to stand right in front of me. "I know you've got a lot going on right now, but about your dad... don't let anyone else's opinion of you determine your self-worth. You mean the world to Levi and to us. You're a good man, and I know it's not from the father you need to hear this from, but if it's approval you want, believe me, you have it right here."

My heart warmed and my eyes filled with tears. I didn't know what to say to that. There were no words except a hugely inadequate tear-filled, snotty, "Thank you."

Levi put his hand up. "Mum, Dad, I love you both dearly, but no more making Harrison cry today, okay?" he said fondly. He kissed both their cheeks and said, "Tell you everything in the morning," before taking my good hand and pulling me up the stairs. And he would tell them everything; it was the kind of relationship they had. I didn't mind at all. Hell, I envied it.

Levi helped me out of my shoes, then my shirt and jeans. He pulled back the covers and waited for me to lay down before joining me. With my broken hand cradled gently between our chests, he kissed the side of my head. "Feel okay?"

I sighed at the warmth of his arms around me. "Better."

"Rough night, huh?"

"Yeah." Then after a long silence, I whispered, "My dad knows."

Levi rubbed my back. "I know."

"I knew he'd find out someday. I just wanted to tell him, that's all. I wanted to tell him how happy you make me, but instead it was a yelling match."

"Oh, babe," he said, planting another kiss on my temple. "He'll come around. Give him some time."

I shook my head and my eyes burned with tears. "I'm sick of fighting it. I'm sick of never being good enough."

Levi took a deep breath and tightened his hold on me. "You *are* good enough. And you're allowed to be angry, Harrison," he murmured. "You're entitled to be disappointed and frustrated and hurt. But don't give up on him yet. I know you, Harrison, and I know, no matter how much you say otherwise, you want his approval. You want him to be proud. You still have hope inside you." He kissed my forehead. "You're better than good enough."

And there was that godforsaken word.

Hope.

I wanted to argue. I wanted to tell him I had had enough, and if my father could walk away, then so could I.

But I was so tired, and even under the chemical buffer the doctor had given me, my hand ached like hell. Even more than that, I couldn't argue because Levi was right. So instead, I cried myself to sleep.

Levi never let me go.

I WOKE up with the headache from hell. Not only did my hand feel like it had been hit with a hammer, my head did too. The bed was empty, though I knew Levi wouldn't be far. No doubt in the kitchen talking to his mum. And that was exactly where I found them.

"Let me make you a cup of tea," Mrs Aston said, busying herself as soon as I walked in.

Levi carefully lifted my splinted hand. "How is it?"

"Sore."

He rolled his eyes. "No swelling, numbness?"

I shook my head. "No. My head hurts."

Levi put his hand to my cheek, as if trying to soothe the ache in my skull. Funnily enough, it did a little. "Stress will do that," he said softly. "I'll get you some ibuprofen."

I sat at the table with my broken, splinted hand against my chest and let them fuss over me. And fuss they did. Levi had told his mum everything, and I was glad I didn't have to repeat it. She kept looking at me with sad eyes. It wasn't pity, it was a recognition that I'd come out to my father and it hadn't gone well. Not that I probably expected it to. But I had hoped.

"Are you still going in for a practice this afternoon?" Levi asked. He put the tablets on the table and sat down with his knee touching mine. He put his hand on my good arm.

"I have to," I said, then swallowed down the pills.

"I'll make you some toast," Mrs Aston said. "You can't be taking pills on an empty stomach. And drink your tea before it goes cold."

Her mother-henning over me made me smile. Most people probably would have hated it, but for me, it was nice.

"Your mum phoned," Levi said gently. He frowned as my smile died. "She asked if you were okay. I didn't say what happened but told her you'd call her later."

I nodded. "Did she mention... *him*?"

"She didn't say whether or not he'd told her what happened, no. If that's what you're asking," he said, squeezing my arm. "Eat your toast, and take a shower. It'll make you feel better. I'm coming to your studio session with you."

I knew there would be no point in arguing but tried anyway. "You have to study."

"I'll bring my books with me. The change of scene will be good, and it's quiet. Apart from the piano of course, but you know I love hearing you play," he said, clearly having it all planned out. "But first we'll need to take that splint off and check for swelling and discolouration. And you will wear it to school and only take it off when you sit at your piano, and the splint goes straight back on after you're done, okay?"

I smiled at him, despite the ache in my chest. "Okay."

Mrs Aston put two slices of toast in front of me and rubbed my shoulder. "Eat up, love."

I managed one slice, washed it down with a mouthful of tea, and pushed the rest of it away. Then Mrs Aston slowly unwrapped the bandage on my hand. The splint was keeping my pinky and ring fingers immobile and together, and taking that off felt both good and painful.

"You've got some great colours happening there," she said.

"And some swelling," Levi added. "How does that feel? Can you move it?"

I straightened out my fingers the best I could. They felt tight, stiff, and really fucking sore. I bit back a grimace and curled my fingers.

"Oh Jesus, Harrison," Levi said. "You can't play today."

I put my hand in my lap, taking it out of view from everyone. "I'll be fine. They're just a bit stiff from being in that splint, that's all." I stood and picked up the plate with my left hand and put it in the sink. "I'll just go have that shower."

Washing myself with my left hand was weird, but drying myself was damn near impossible. I was standing in the bathroom with no more than a towel around my waist, contemplating how the hell I was going to put on underwear or jeans when Levi knocked on the door. "Babe?"

"Yeah? You can come in."

He let himself in and closed the door behind him. He eyed my still wet chest and ogled my towel-covered crotch. "Normally I'd be all over that," he said with a smirk. "But given you're injured, I thought I'd come and see if you needed some help."

"Ugh," I groaned, looking at my stupid broken hand. "It's such a pain."

Levi ran the hot water and filled the bathroom sink. He took a spare towel and dried my chest and back, then ruffled it through my hair before hanging it over my shoulder. "Come on then," he said, grabbing the shaving foam. "I'll give you a shave."

"I could probably do it," I reasoned.

Levi rolled his eyes. "You're not shaving with your left

hand. It'll be bad enough you turn up tomorrow with your hand as it is. You're not looking like Freddy Krueger as well."

It made me smile.

"And just so you know," he went on, as he lathered my face with shaving foam, "I'm doing this because I love you. Not because I pity you. There's a difference, you know."

"I know, thank you."

"Don't talk," he said, putting the razor to my cheek near my ear. "And anyway, the same goes for my mum and dad. They love you, Harrison."

"I know."

"Don't talk," he said, his eyes narrowing at my jaw as he scraped the razor down the skin. "Mum doesn't want you to feel like she's pestering you, but she wanted you to know that you have a home here. For as long as you need it."

I let out a slow breath. "Your parents are really great, you know that?"

He huffed. "I said don't talk. I'll end up slicing your face, and you're too pretty to have a scar from your ear to your mouth."

"Too pretty?"

Levi scoffed and rolled his eyes. "There's a mirror there, try looking in it. You're gorgeous. But you know this right? Well," he amended, "I've told you a hundred times, but whether or not you see what I see is anyone's guess."

He stared into my eyes for a long moment and his shoulders fell. "You really don't, do you?"

I stared at the wall, anywhere else but the mirror or at Levi. "Are we nearly done?"

Levi finished shaving me, lifting and turning my chin as he needed, and eventually he rinsed me off and patted me dry. I put my left hand to his chest. "Thank you," I told him.

"Harrison." He said my name so it sounded almost musical. "You're very welcome. I'd do anything for you."

I rested my forehead against his. "How did I get so lucky?"

He smiled and gave me a quick kiss. "I could ask myself the same question. Come on, I'll help you get dressed. And if you're really lucky, I'll even let you give me a quick blowjob for my efforts."

I snorted out a laugh. "How generous of you."

"Oh, shut up," he said with a snort. "You know damn well you're not getting underpants on until I've had you in my mouth." He opened the bathroom door and led me to our room where we did exactly that.

CHAPTER 12

IT HAD TAKEN Levi to help me get dressed, and both Levi and Mrs Aston made sure my hand was properly splinted. And with a new dose of painkillers, we set off for my college.

I hid my hand and thankfully got to my studio unseen. Levi helped unwrap my hand and left me at the piano, sat himself in a chair in the corner, and put his nose in a book. He was supposed to be studying, though I knew he would spend most of the two hours watching me.

I sat at the piano and put my hands to the keys. My right hand throbbed, and how a pain could be both dull and sharp at the same time, I'd never know. Trying to compartmentalise it, trying to put the pain into some box in my mind and shutting it away, I took a deep breath and started to play.

My hand recoiled as soon as I'd stretched my pinky finger and a stabbing pain shot through my hand and up my arm.

Fuck.

I bit back a cry and took another deep breath, glancing

straight at Levi, who, thankfully, didn't seem to have caught it. I needed to do this. I needed to put the pain aside and do this. I *could* do this. I knew I had it in me. I had to prove it not only to my parents—who for all I knew where on a plane back to Australia—not just to Levi and his parents, but to myself as well.

And so, I imagined this performance was for my life. I imagined that it all hung on this very piece. My life here, my happiness, living with Levi and his family. It all came down to this. And in many ways, I guess it did.

I closed my eyes, took a deep breath, and played.

THERE'S a line between tolerable and intolerable pain. And when you get to that line, it is possible to push it back just a little further each time. There's a pain threshold you can get past where it hurts like hell, but you can keep doing what you're doing and the pain doesn't get any worse.

That's where I was at. Until I stopped playing.

I managed to do the two hours, but when I took my hands from the keys, the pain got exponentially worse.

"Two hours was too long," Levi said. "You're sweating and you're pale." He took my hand and quickly put the splint back on and wrapped the bandage around it to keep it in place.

I laughed, which sounded a little maniacal. "You know how I said it hurt before?"

Levi looked at me and nodded.

"Well that wasn't hurting."

Levi grabbed his bag and took my other arm, urging me to my feet. "Come on. I'm taking you back to the hospital."

I stopped. "No. They won't tell us what we don't already know. I overused it, that's all."

"Harrison," he started.

I shook my head. "I'll be fine. I'm done now. We'll go home and I'll rest it, ice it and it'll be fine."

He didn't look pleased, so I reasoned, "If, after the exam tomorrow, it's no better we'll go back to the doctor. I promise."

Levi scowled at me. "For the record, I think this is crazy. And I think you're a stubborn... Ugh." He shook his head at me, and his voice was softer when he spoke next. "I know why you're doing it, and I get that. I really do. But if you have to defer for a year, people will understand. Just because you can't sit this exam, doesn't mean you fail, Harrison. It doesn't mean it all ends here. There will be more chances. Your masterclass professor said you're the most naturally talented pianist she's seen in years. She'll understand. You broke your hand, Harrison. It's not like you just woke up and didn't want to play anymore."

I put my finger to his lips to make him stop talking, then I kissed him softly. "Thank you."

He sighed with relief. "Does that mean you'll call them and tell them you can't sit the exam?"

I smiled at him. "Of course not. Don't be silly. Let's go home."

He grumbled under his breath until we walked out onto Marylebone Road.

"Harrison?" a familiar voice called.

I turned to find one of my professors walking into the building. "Professor Patelli," I answered.

"Everything okay?" he asked, looking directly at my hand.

"Oh sure," I replied quickly. "Just getting in my final practice."

He took the four steps down to us. "You're injured."

"I am," I said, lifting my hand. There was no point in denying it. "But I'll be fine for tomorrow."

He was frowning, still staring at my hand. "If you are unable—"

"I'm fine," I interrupted. "I'm playing tomorrow."

"Hmm." He clearly disapproved. "Very well."

I SAT ONCE AGAIN at the kitchen table. It really was the central hub of the Aston house. Levi's brother, sister and father were there, trying not to fuss too much but they kept asking me if I was okay while Levi held a bag of frozen peas on my hand. Mrs Aston was at work and it was so weird that I felt better when she got home soon after. "Let me make you some tea," she said, and had a cup in my good hand in no time. She put two painkillers on the table as well. "Take those."

"Thank you," I told her. She replied with a kiss to the top of my head, then proceeded to organise dinner while talking with everyone. It was a loud household, especially around dinnertime when everyone was there. It was so different to what I was used to. As there was noise and bustling around us, I looked at Levi and smiled. "Love you," I mouthed.

He smiled, an almost shy smirk. It wasn't a look he wore often.

And then, landing back in reality with a resounding thud, my phone rang. "It's my mother," I said, reading the screen.

"Want me to talk to her," Mrs Aston offered.

With a long sigh, I shook my head. "No, thank you. I'll talk to her."

I answered the call as I walked to our room, knowing, hoping Levi would follow. Of course he did. "Hi, Mum."

"Oh, Harrison," she said. "Are you okay?"

"I'm fine. Did you get your sightseeing in today?" I asked.

There was a beat of silence. "Your father told me you had a disagreement."

My silence matched hers. "Is that all he said?" I asked finally, wondering if he told her I'd come out to him.

"Harrison," she said softly. "I just want to know you're okay."

"I'm fine," I lied. "Super."

"I understand you need to rest and study tonight, so I won't ask you to dinner."

I almost snorted. *Yeah, sure that was the reason.* "Yeah."

"We'll see you tomorrow, though," she finished. "And Harrison?"

"Yes?"

"Good luck."

I disconnected the call and fell back onto the bed. My hand fucking ached. My head and heart weren't much better. I closed my eyes and waited for the pain meds to kick in. The last thing I remembered was Levi kissing my forehead and pulling the blankets up.

The next thing I knew, it was morning. And my exam came around quicker than I thought possible. I kept myself distracted, trying not to overthink, but the ache in my chest and the sharp pain in my hand was a heavy reminder of everything that had happened.

Oddly enough, I wasn't nervous. I knew this music

piece like I knew my own name. I'd played it so much I could do it in my sleep. My fingers knew each bar, every note, every nuance, like it was muscle memory.

Levi unstrapped the bandage and took the splint off my hand. "Harrison, no matter what happens in there, one hour from now you will still be perfect to me. I don't care if you go in there and nail it or say you can't do it. I'll love you regardless." He took a deep breath and straightened up. "Now go in there and do what you do."

If I could have walked straight out onto the floor and played right away, I think I'd have been fine. But I had to wait forty minutes, and that's a really bloody long time to get lost in your own head. Every conversation I'd ever had with my father about how insignificant playing the piano was rambled through my mind. Years of being told my dreams were foolish slinked through my memories, and the way I felt each time my father shot me down.

Then there was the time I'd played the piano for my parents in that restaurant in Sydney, and my father told me I needed to play, that I should be heard. The hope I'd felt, the joy at his approval, the relief... the hope.

Then his face the other night, our fight in the street, and the broken bones in my hand that reminded me that maybe, just maybe, I wouldn't ever get his approval, that I wouldn't ever be good enough.

And it was with that thought... that weight—the heaviest of hearts—I walked out on stage to play my final exam.

THERE WERE professors sitting down at the front tables and about twenty chairs behind them, the audience full and waiting. I saw Levi, of course, my eyes trained straight to him. But he was sitting next to Holly, who smiled brightly at me, and next to her sat my mother and father. I swallowed down the lump in my throat and almost tripped on my way to the piano. Flooded with nervousness and dread, I took my seat, and with a deep breath, I centred myself.

I don't know where it came from, I don't know what made me do it. Maybe it was the ache in my heart and the pain in my hand, but I focused on that.

The music piece I was to play was Beethoven's Sonata no. 26; *Les Adieu*. A deep, sorrowful, heart-broken song. A musical masterpiece that was enriched by tones of anger and frustration, loss and absence, but tinged with hope.

It always came back to hope.

Eighteen minutes of excruciating pain in my hand, compounded by eighteen years of pain in my heart, each note of hurt and hope came from my very soul. In that moment, that piece was the story of my life, and I played with such emotion, such perfection, like I'd never played before. I put my heart on display for the world to see.

It wasn't until it was over that I realised tears had slid down my face. There was a long pause of silence before Levi and Holly were on their feet, applauding in an otherwise silent room. It wasn't exam room etiquette to clap, and it made me smile. The professors looked pleased with how I played, nodding to one another.

I'd done it. I'd gotten through it. My first year was over: the hard work, the stress. I'd done the best I could do, and if that was good enough, only time would tell.

My knuckles felt like there was a knife of fire twisted between them. With a shaky breath, I wiped my cheeks with my left hand and slowly stood up. I cradled my hand and kept my eyes on the professors, avoiding eye contact with my parents just a few seats away. I bowed my head to the adjudicators and turned to make my leave.

"Mr Haddon?" Professor Millard called. "Your hand? You are injured?"

I stopped and faced them, giving him a nod. I held up my purple and swollen hand. "I broke it."

"You played Beethoven with a broken hand?" a visiting professor, whose name I didn't know, asked.

I gave a single nod. "I did, yes."

The faculty staff looked between themselves, some with raised eyebrows, some with smiles. "It was quite a performance," Professor Patelli said.

"I had quite the mentor," I replied with a smile.

"Failure just isn't an option for you, is it Mr Haddon?"

I could feel my father's eyes on me, though I gave my professor my full attention. "No, sir. It's not."

"Very well," he replied with an amused look. And with that, I was dismissed.

I made my way through the stage door, to the outdoor courtyard. I passed Jure, a Croatian student, and wished him well before Donna and a group of friends surrounded me asking, "How was it? How did you play? What were they like?"

"Oh my God," Donna said. "Your hand! Harrison, it's purple!"

I laughed. "I uh, I broke it."

They all stared at me. "And you still performed?"

"Of course," I said. "I had to."

"You're crazy!"

Then after a dozen rapid-fire questions about how it happened, how much it hurt, how long until it's healed, someone tapped me on the shoulder. I turned to find Levi with the proudest smile I'd ever seen on his face. He pulled me against him and hugged me so tight, my sore hand hanging out to the side. When he let me go, he took my face in his hands and kissed me. "I'm so proud of you," he said. "You fucking nailed it. Harrison, you nailed it!"

I nodded. "I did okay, yeah?"

"Okay? It was perfect! I bet Beethoven himself couldn't play it like that."

It was then I noticed Holly was standing beside us. Before I could even think that Levi had kissed me in front of her, she threw her arms around me. "Harrison, it was remarkable. You were remarkable!"

I didn't know how much her approval meant to me until she said that. I squeezed her. "Thank you." I turned to face my friends and, with my arm still around Holly, I introduced her. "This is my sister, Holly. And these are my friends."

A quick burst of questions went around about her trip from Sydney, how she was liking London, what instruments they studied, when I noticed Levi looking over my shoulder. I turned to see who he was looking at, though part of me already knew.

My mother and father stood back, watching us and smiling nervously, looking terribly out of place, and I knew I couldn't put this off any longer.

We said goodbye to the others, leaving just the five of us. No one knew where to look and no one knew where to start.

So Levi took the splint and bandage and handed it to my father, then he slipped his arm through Holly's, saying something about getting some coffees. "Mrs Haddon, care to join us?"

My mother nodded, but then looked up at me. Her eyes glistened with unshed tears. "You played beautifully. I'm incredibly proud of you," she said.

"Thank you." And I truly meant it. Her words warmed my heart.

My father and I watched the three of them leave, and he held up the splint and bandage. "You broke your hand," he said. It wasn't a question.

"Uh, yeah."

"How is it?"

"Sore."

"I bet it is," he said. "I can't imagine how deep you had to dig to get through that exam." He swallowed hard. "It was everything your mother said, only more. Hearing you play that, watching you... I am very proud of you."

Oh.

Oh.

I cleared my throat. "Um, thank you. That means a lot." Then of course I had to go ruin it by trying to run my hand through my hair. I pulled my hand back and cried out, "Ow! Shit."

"Want me to take a look at it?"

I didn't really but figured olive branches should go in both directions. "Sure."

I held out my hand and he took it in his. I couldn't remember a time, even as a child, when he ever held my hand. But his surgeon fingers were gentle but firm as he turned my hand and lightly skimmed the purple skin that covered from the knuckles to the wrist. I grimaced as he touched a sensitive spot. "You hit something," he said.

"I punched a streetlight," I admitted. I felt childish telling him that.

He frowned. "The other night?"

I nodded. "Yeah."

"Harrison, I really am sorry," he said softly, genuinely. "For how I reacted."

He looked as uncomfortable as I felt, but this was it. Some part of me knew that this conversation would either make us or break us. As much as we struggled to communicate, we needed to try. "I'm sorry too," I said. "I didn't want you to find out that way. I should have told you."

He shook his head. "No. You should have told us only when you were ready." He looked out across the garden. "I'll admit it was a bit of a shock."

"I love him."

His eyes shot to mine, and after the longest moment he nodded. "I can see that."

"He's the best thing to ever happen to me."

My father smiled, somewhat awkwardly, but nodded toward a bench seat. "Wanna sit down?"

"Sure."

We sat in the London sun, as some familiar faces walked past with books under their arms and a smile in my direction.

"You like it here?" he asked.

"I love it," I told him. "I fit in here, Dad. The professors are great. The college is awesome. The people are... well, they're like me. There's no group of footballers trying to flush my head down the toilet here."

His eyes flashed to mine. "Did they? Back home? Try and do that?"

"Once or twice," I admitted with a shrug.

"Why didn't you tell us?" he asked.

I laughed, but there was no humour in it. He nodded in understanding. Then he said, "Can I tell you a story?" He didn't wait for my answer, he just kept talking. "Twenty-five years ago, there was a kid—a man," he amended, "not much older than you. He was in med school and he worked night-shifts, packing shelves at a supermarket to pay his way. He got by on almost no sleep, very little money, and he ran himself into the ground. He had a new wife and a lifetime of pressure from his father to be the best doctor he could be."

He took a deep breath and exhaled slowly. "After his third year, after working his job, then doing a fourteen hour residency stint, he was so exhausted he passed out in a lecture study. One of his professors called him in and told him something had to give. Before he suggested a leave of absence, he asked why. Why do that to yourself?"

I looked at my father. "What did you tell him?"

He smiled. "I told him *exactly* what you just told your professor in there," he nodded toward the building. "Failure is not an option."

"Must be a Haddon family trait," I said.

My father didn't smile. "I did fail, Harrison. I failed my most important job." He swallowed hard and let out a shaky breath. "I failed at being a father, and I failed you."

I looked at him then. Really looked at him. I noticed, for probably the first time, the grey hair at his temples, the wrinkles on his face, the sadness in his eyes.

He shook his head. "I have held people's hearts in my hand. Strangers. I've spent my life fixing the hearts of strangers, yet I couldn't even acknowledge the damage I'd done to yours. And I'm more sorry for that than you can imagine."

I blinked back tears. "It's possible I was a spoiled brat."

He barked out a laugh. "No, Harrison. You tried telling me time and time again what you wanted, and I didn't listen. I can see that now." He frowned deeply. "Everything you said the other night was true. All the money and privilege in the world counts for naught when you only wanted five minutes of my time."

So while he was putting his cards on the table, I laid mine out as well. "I grew up alone, Dad. It was hard growing up and being kept at arm's length, even as a little kid. I felt very detached and very alone. Sorry if that hurts to hear, but it's the truth. Then to realise I would only disappoint you further because I didn't want to be a doctor, but it was the one thing I couldn't lie to myself about. It was hard enough hiding the fact I'm gay. I mean, maybe I pushed not becoming a doctor so hard because it was the one disappointment I thought you could possibly live with."

He shook his head. "What do you mean, live with?"

"You know, not kick me out for."

His eyes went wide. "No, Harrison. I'd never have kicked you out."

"How was I to know that?" I asked. Tears filled my eyes. "All you ever told me was that unless I was the doctor you wanted me to be, I'd never be good enough."

"You aren't a disappointment, Harrison. You never were." He swallowed hard. "I'm sorry if I ever said that or implied it. I'm very proud of you. Your mother and I both are. You stood up for what you wanted. You're living in London, going to the music school of your dreams. There's not many people who have the balls to do that."

I almost smiled. "You said your father wanted you to be the best doctor. Did Grandad pressure you?"

"Oh yeah." My father sighed. "And to think I did the same to you."

"Did you want to be something else?"

He looked at me and smiled. "No. Not ever. It was all I ever dreamed of."

"It's what Holly wants," I told him. "You know that, right? She wants to do pre-med next year."

He smiled at that. "I do know. Well, after you asked me

the other night if I had any idea what she wanted to do, it made me realise I didn't have a clue. So we sat down yesterday and talked. Actually, we talked a lot."

"I'm glad to hear that."

"Harrison, I hope you don't mind, but I told your mum and sister that you and Levi... are an item."

I snorted. "An *item*?"

"A couple," he amended with an embarrassed smile. "I realise it wasn't my place to tell them, but they wanted to know what we fought over. They ganged up on me and I caved in. I'm sorry. It was your secret to tell, not mine."

"It's okay, Dad," I said. And it was. Actually, I was relieved it wasn't a secret any more. "I'm pretty sure Holly knew."

He nodded. "She said she did. She likes Levi. Said he's a good guy."

"He is. He's great. His family's great. They have literally taken me in like I'm one of them. His dad makes me watch soccer—sorry, football—and his mum feeds me toast and tea every time she sees me. Which is great, except I haven't had the courage to tell her that Marmite is shit compared to Vegemite."

Dad laughed at that. "I'll post you some."

I smiled at him. "I'd really appreciate that."

It was then he realised he was still holding my splint. "Want me to put this on?"

"Yeah, that'd be great," I answered. "Thanks."

Then, without another word between us, he skilfully applied the splint and wrapped the bandage around my hand just as Levi, Holly, and my mother returned. Levi eyed me cautiously but seemed pleased that my father and I were smiling and not trying to kill each other. I gave him a smile that told him it was okay. He was holding a takeout coffee tray with two coffees and held them out to us.

I took the cup with my left hand. "How's your hand?" Mum asked.

"It's okay," I said. Then I resolved to be more honest with them. "Sore as hell, actually."

Levi looked at his watch. "You can't have any more ibuprofen for another three hours. Do you want to go home and ice it?"

I shook my head. "Nah. I'm sure it'll be fine." Then I lifted my arm in an open invitation, which Levi accepted.

For the first time in front of my family, they were privy to me openly showing affection to another man. He slid into the crook of my arm and put his arm around my waist. "Can I just say," he said, "your exam performance was brilliant, broken hand and all."

"I agree," my mother said, smiling at me. "In fact, I was telling Levi and Holly before that I heard one of the professors say it was the best finals performance they'd seen all week."

"Oh," I said, and a flush of pride filled my chest.

My father smiled and sighed deeply. It was the sound of relief, like a weight lifted. "So, shall we do lunch? My treat."

"I'd like that," I said. So the five of us walked out of my college together.

As we walked down the street, Levi whispered, "Everything went okay with your dad, then?"

I smiled at him. "It's not perfect," I answered, so only he could hear. "There's still some things we'll need to get over."

His smile lit up his whole face. "But it's a start."

I found myself grinning. "Yeah. I think it is."

EPILOGUE

THREE YEARS LATER

I OPENED the door to our place. It was a two-bedroom townhouse, narrow and not overly huge, but it was ours. Well, ours to rent. We were a while off being able to afford a place in London on our own. Like maybe a lifetime away, but it didn't matter. Levi and I were just happy to finally be living on our own.

I couldn't deny it had been a trying three years. Both of us students with pending stresses and financial concerns, but we made it through. I was in my finals week. My bachelor's degree was coming down to two more exams. I'd been at college all morning, practicing for hours. One-on-one sessions with Professor Patelli were gruelling, but amazing at the same time. Though, like every year at finals time, my mind wandered to my parents.

The last three years with them had been... better. Not perfect—I don't think any one of us ever pretended it would be— but we talked more. Levi and I had been to visit them in Sydney once, and they'd been to London one other time, but our communications were mostly limited to phone calls and emails. And sometimes that was a good thing. Working on the whole 'learning to talk to one another' thing was actually more effective when we spoke without seeing each other. We made the effort to actually talk because it was the only thing we could do. We weren't the Brady Bunch by any stretch of the imagination, but I had to admit I was disappointed when my parents said they couldn't make it to my graduation. They'd missed some pretty important performances, here and overseas, but I'd hoped they'd be able to watch me graduate.

I understood. I truly did. My father did important work. Some growing up on my part made me realise that. I wouldn't dismiss how much I hated his commitment to his job when I was younger, but now at twenty-two years of age I had a little more perspective than my eighteen-year-old self did.

Twenty-two wasn't old and wise, at all. But a few more years' perspective helped. Maybe I just had a little more appreciation for his level of dedication. Either way, I think we understood each other a little better.

"Hey, I'm home," I called out as I put my satchel on the floor near the front door. I expected Levi to be upstairs studying, or with his books all over the dining table. But he wasn't. He was standing in the lounge room with an envelope in his hand. "Hey," I said again, eyeing him cautiously. "What's up?"

He held out the envelope. My name was handwritten on the front, the insignia was one I recognised immediately. St Michael's Private Boys School, Sydney. "What is it?" I asked.

"Open it," he said.

I pulled out the letter and started to read.

MR HARRISON HADDON,

As a former student of this school, and as an internationally acclaimed student of music, we would be honoured to have you as a guest speaker. Discussing matters such as the cultural importance of student exchange programs.

I LOOKED UP AT LEVI. "What...? How...?"

"They must have heard that you performed in New York," he said.

I showed him the envelope. "No, it's not stamped. How did you get this?"

My father stepped out from the kitchen. He smiled at my stunned expression. "Hand-delivered."

My first reaction was one of shock, and then to hug him. I think I shocked him too as I pulled him in for a tight embrace, but man, it was good to see him. Mum was there too, hiding in the kitchen, and I gave her a hug too. "Holly wishes she could be here," Mum told me.

"I know," I said. "She's swamped. A double-degree at med school will do that." Then I looked at Levi. "You kept this from me?"

He laughed. "It wasn't easy."

I looked at my parents, who were genuinely happy to see me. Happy for me, for me and my boyfriend. "I'm so glad you guys are here."

Dad smiled the eye-crinkling kind of smile. "Wouldn't have missed it."

"How long are you staying for?" I asked.

"A week," Mum replied.

"We didn't want to miss your graduation," Dad said. "It's not every day you graduate with honours from one of the most acclaimed music schools in the world."

His words, and the pride with which he spoke them, sent a rush of warmth through my chest. "Thank you. It really means a lot."

"When do you start your Masters?"

"Pre courses in six weeks," I answered.

"Good," Dad replied. "Just enough time."

"For what?" I asked, curious at his smirk.

"We have an appointment two days after your graduation at Steinway & Sons," he replied simply. "Did you know they custom make pianos? I had no idea. Order turn around and delivery is five to six weeks."

I stared at him. Then I blinked. "What?"

His smile became a grin. "It's your graduation present."

My mouth fell open, and I shook my head. "No."

My father nodded. "Appointment's been made."

I spun to Levi. "Did you know about this?"

He shook his head. Truthfully, his shocked expression should have told me he was innocent in this. "Not at all."

"We don't have the room here," I said, still trying to get my head around the generous offer.

"It'll fit," my father replied.

Levi slid his arm around my waist. "We'll make it fit."

I couldn't believe it. "And St Michael's wants me to be a guest speaker?" My head was spinning. "Which means a trip back to Sydney." I looked at Levi. "How can we fit that in? Our schedules are crazy, and not to mention affording it."

Levi's smile was slow and spreading. He rubbed his hand on my back, which he knew helped me calm down. "Harrison, we'll make it work."

"I'm not even the expert on the student exchange program," I argued.

"Well, you certainly reaped the benefits of it," Levi said.

I burst out laughing. "True. I did." Both my mum and dad smiled at that, and I still couldn't believe they were here. "And a Steinway piano?"

"We missed you playing in New York," Dad said. "We've missed a lot in your life so far, and this is not some attempt to buy a fix for all those years, Harrison. Think of it as more of a...." He searched for the right word.

"An acceptance of my music?" I suggested.

Dad sighed with a smile. "More than that. How many hours do you spend away from home practicing?"

"A lot," Levi answered for me.

"Now you don't have to leave," he said softly. "I spent far too many hours away from home. And that is time I can't ever get back. You know that better than anyone. I don't want you to make the same mistake." He looked at Levi, then back to me. "Don't take the ones you love for granted. You taught me that, Harrison. So consider this my thanks for the reminder of what's truly important."

My eyes filled with tears, but I blinked them back with a laugh. I hugged my father, and he held me just as tight. Eventually he pulled back. "I hope you don't mind," he said, "but I asked Levi's parents if they'd like to join us for dinner."

"I don't mind at all," I replied. "In fact, I think it'll be perfect." I found myself back in front of Levi. "Thank you," I whispered.

He searched my eyes. "What for?"

"Years ago in our school dorm room, you filled in the application that brought me here. You made me believe in myself." I kissed him softly. "And I got so much more than just music."

He smiled the eye-crinkling kind of smile that still gave me butterflies. "I got you too," he said.

I replied with his usual line to me: his promise to me, I gave back to him. "Two four seven, three six five."

~THE END

ABOUT THE AUTHOR

N.R. Walker is an Australian author, who loves her genre of gay romance. She loves writing and spends far too much time doing it, but wouldn't have it any other way.

She is many things: a mother, a wife, a sister, a writer. She has pretty, pretty boys who live in her head, who don't let her sleep at night unless she gives them life with words.

She likes it when they do dirty, dirty things... but likes it even more when they fall in love.

She used to think having people in her head talking to her was weird, until one day she happened across other writers who told her it was normal.

She's been writing ever since...

ALSO BY N.R. WALKER

The Weight Of It All

Switched

Point of No Return

Breaking Point

Starting Point

Spencer Cohen Book One

Spencer Cohen Book Two

Spencer Cohen Book Three

Yanni's Story

On Davis Row

Free Reads:

Sixty Five Hours

Learning to Feel

His Grandfather's Watch (And The Story of Billy and Hale)

The Twelfth of Never (Blind Faith 3.5)

Twelve Days of Christmas (Sixty Five Hours Christmas)

Best of Both Worlds

Translated Titles:

Fiducia Cieca (Italian translation of Blind Faith)

Attraverso Questi Occhi (Italian translation of Through These Eyes)

Preso alla Sprovvista (Italian translation of Blindside)

Il giorno del Mai (Italian translation of *Blind Faith 3.5*)

Cuore di Terra Rossa (Italian translation of *Red Dirt Heart*)

Cuore di Terra Rossa 2 (Italian translation of *Red Dirt Heart 2*)

Cuore di Terra Rossa 3 (Italian translation of *Red Dirt Heart 3*)

Cuore di Terra Rossa 4 (Italian translation of *Red Dirt Heart 4*)

Intervento di Retrofit (Italian translation of *Elements of Retrofit*)

Confiance Aveugle (French translation of *Blind Faith*)

A travers ces yeux: Confiance Aveugle 2 (French translation of *Through These Eyes*)

Aveugle: Confiance Aveugle 3 (French translation of *Blindside*)

À Jamais (French translation of *Blind Faith 3.5*)

Cronin's Key (French translation)

Cronin's Key II (French translation)

Au Coeur de Sutton Station (French translation of *Red Dirt Heart*)

Partir ou rester (French translation of *Red Dirt Heart 2*)

Faire Face (French translation of *Red Dirt Heart 3*)

Trouver sa Place (French translation of *Red Dirt Heart 4*)

Rote Erde (German translation of *Red Dirt Heart*)

Rote Erde 2 (German translation of *Red Dirt Heart 2*)

Printed in July 2019
by Rotomail Italia S.p.A., Vignate (MI) - Italy